Leo brought her down on his lap and she straddled him.

She shifted, but he stopped her. "Not yet. I want the chance to explore every part of you in case I screw up later."

She put her hands on either side of his face and looked into his eyes. There was a honesty there that ripped right through her. "I want that, too. You won't screw up."

"Don't. I'm not sure what I'm doing right now. I just know that I can't let you go," he said. He pulled her head down to his, his tongue pushing deep into her mouth. She reached down to take him into her hand and pushed her hips forward and down until she was impaled on him. She stayed still. This was what she'd needed.

"Now you can take your time," she whispered in his ear.

* * *

The One from the Wedding by Katherine Garbera is part of the Destination Wedding series.

Dear Reader,

I'm so excited for you to read Danni and Leo's story. Have you ever said something off the cuff and had the remark come back to bite you? I hate to admit it but I definitely have. Usually, it's more along the lines of "I don't get Ed Sheeran" and then a few weeks later I love "Tenerife Sea." But in this case, it's Leo showing his ego and being more than a little bit arrogant and saying that Danni's small business is just one of many imitators trying to ride his coattails. Um, yeah, that would make me totally ticked off.

Also, if you've ever met me, you might be thinking, "Kathy, you're not that bold." You're totally right, but in my mind I am. And Danni is a lot bolder than I am. She's got one year to make her small business work or she's going to have to go back to being a lawyer, something she's good at and pays the bills but doesn't really love. So, when she sees Leo at the wedding, she's not holding back.

If you've been following the Destination Wedding series you know a few Bisset-family skeletons have come out of the closet, so Leo is glad for the distraction of Danni—not only her boldness in calling him on his arrogance but also the fact that she's smoking hot. Just what he needs for the weekend.

I hope you enjoy returning to Adler and Nick's wedding and Nantucket.

Happy reading!

Katherine

KATHERINE GARBERA

—

THE ONE FROM THE WEDDING

As always thanks to my girl gang, the Zombie Belles—Eve,
Nancy, Lenora, Janet and Denise. I feel so blessed to
have you in my life, and love that you always have my back
and know that I always have yours.

DESIRE™

Recycling programs
for this product may
not exist in your area.

ISBN-13: 978-1-335-73555-3

The One from the Wedding

Copyright © 2022 by Katherine Garbera

This edition published by arrangement with Harlequin Books S.A.

For questions and comments about the quality of this book,
please contact us at CustomerService@Harlequin.com.

Harlequin Enterprises ULC
22 Adelaide St. West, 41st Floor
Toronto, Ontario M5H 4E3, Canada
www.Harlequin.com

Printed in U.S.A.

Katherine Garbera is the *USA TODAY* bestselling author of more than 120 books. She started her career twenty-five years ago at Harlequin Desire writing about strong alpha heroes and feisty heroines and crafting stories that resonate with emotional impact and strong sensuality. She's a Florida girl who has traveled the US, calling different states her home before crossing the pond to settle in the midlands of the UK, where she lives with her husband and a spoiled miniature dachshund. Find her on the web at www.katherinegarbera.com.

You can also find Katherine Garbera on Facebook, along with other Harlequin Desire authors, at Facebook.com/harlequindesireauthors!

To Courtney and Lucas.
I have always felt so lucky to be your mom
and never more so as I've seen the adults
you've become. Love you.

One

"I can't believe you told that magazine my start-up was just trying to ride your coattails."

It was a sunny Friday in June, the first big day of his maternal cousin Adler Osborn's televised Nantucket wedding weekend. Well, the first public day; Leo and his family had been on Nantucket for two days now. Two very eventful days, in which an explosive revelation involving Leo's father and the groom's mother had nearly derailed the entire wedding.

They'd all convened at today's golf scramble and were keeping up a brave front. But Leo's mom looked like she'd aged ten years overnight. His bubbly cousin, the bride-to-be, was forcing her smile and looked like she was ready to snap. He'd been hoping today's round of golf would be a relief from the pressure they'd all been under.

Seeing as how he'd been assigned to play with an upstart business competitor whom he'd dissed in an interview not more than a month ago, he guessed that wasn't going to be the case. He knew that Adler had commissioned Danni Eldridge to make the brides-maids' jewelry instead of him because they were friends from school. But Adler had then asked Leo to supply the grooms' gifts. His line of handcrafted leather goods fit the bill perfectly.

He had no idea what Danni looked like before this moment. Her online accounts simply had her name and an old-fashioned Singer sewing machine logo for a profile picture. Seeing her now, he wouldn't say she was classically beautiful but something about her made him take notice. She was to be the fourth in their team for the scramble so he wanted to smooth things over.

Leo had never met someone he couldn't charm. He put his hand over his heart and gave the woman a humble look. "Please accept my most profound apology. Sometimes I get a little cranky when I'm bombarded with questions from journalists and just answer off the cuff. I never would have said it if we'd had the chance to meet before. Can we please start over?"

She watched him with dark brown eyes, and he

had a feeling that his apology wasn't really sooth-ing her ire. He didn't blame her at all. If someone had said that about his business, he'd never have forgiven them.

"I guess we should. Otherwise this foursome is going to be pretty awkward," she said with a genu-ine and sincere smile. "I'm Danni Eldridge. I'm at the wedding because I designed the bridesmaids' jewelry and Adler is a friend of mine."

"Leo Bisset. Adler's my cousin," he said, offering his hand. "Pleased to meet you."

They shook, and he couldn't help but notice how delicate her hand felt in his. Her nails were mani-cured but in a subtle shade. Not the latest trendy nail color that he'd seen all over his social feed from followers and influencers. Her perfume was subtle and reminded him of sunshine and days spent at the beach. She pulled her hand away and then turned to the golf cart where his brother and mom were waiting.

"So I'm going to be the only one in this group who doesn't know everyone," she said. "Tell me what I need to know."

"What do you want to know?" Leo asked. "My brother Logan is very competitive, but I'm slightly better than he is, and my mom is the nicest woman I know. She'll keep Logan in line if he acts up."

Danni smiled and shook her head. "Who's going to keep you in line?"

He winked at her. "No one can, unfortunately. But I'll try to be on my best behavior to make up for that horrible thing I said."

"You think that will work?" she asked.

"Not really, but I'm hoping you'll give me a break since you know I'm trying," he said. He'd found that honesty was always the best way to make up with anyone he'd offended. He had to admit this wasn't the first time he'd said something that had upset a woman he was attracted to. He wasn't really concerned about smaller businesses moving into the classic luxury lifestyle marketplace. He had always believed that a rising tide raised all ships, and he was captaining a big old fleet of luxury yachts, so he felt secure.

"Do you just do jewelry? I wonder why that journalist brought you up in the Q and A."

She shook her head. "I make nautical-themed bracelets and watchbands. Some people have said the quality and craftsmanship is on par with yours."

He doubted that. He had a crew of highly skilled workers who had been with him since the beginning. He'd always known he couldn't be the heir to the throne at Bisset Industries, an American multinational corporation involved in the manufacturing, refining and distribution of petroleum, chemicals, energy, minerals, fertilizers, pulp and paper, chemical technology equipment, ranching, finance, commodities trading and investing—that was going to his older brother Logan. So Leo had struck out and made his own way from the ground up. He'd taken the time to learn how to make the leather goods that he'd first sold at craft fairs and then in a thriving mail-order business that he'd grown from his on-line followers and now sold in a flagship store in the Hamptons. Leo had grown the company into a lifestyle brand that had gone global. He'd worked hard for everything he had, and while he appreciated that Danni thought her product was as nice as his, he doubted that she was hand-making every item. Many small crafters relied on imports and cheaply made designs.

"Are you wearing your product?" he asked, glancing down at her wrist and noticing the metal-and-grosgrain-ribbon bracelet that had a small *D* charm with an anchor wrapped around it.

"I am," she said, holding up her wrist.

He noticed how small and delicate her bones were, but then he looked more closely at the bracelet and saw how well-made it was. "May I?"

She unclasped it and handed it over to him. He had to admit that it was on par with if not better than some of the ones he carried in his store. But making one nice bracelet wasn't the same as manufacturing a large quantity of high-quality goods. He handed it back to her.

"I like it. I can only guess that I hadn't seen your product when I made my remark," he said. "Hopefully while we're playing, I can show you that I'm not the arrogant guy you must believe me to be."

"We'll see. I did hear you challenging your brother, and you sounded pretty arrogant."

"That's not fair. Logan was being…well, Logan," Leo said. "Do you have siblings?"

"Yes," she said. "An older brother and sister."

"Then you know what I mean. They can be very trying," he said.

She laughed. "I have to agree. It's just funny to think of Logan Bisset as a pesky older brother."

"Trust me, he is very…pesky," Leo said. "But I, on the other hand, am pretty charming."

"Pretty charming? I assume you're talking about me," Logan said as he rejoined them.

"Hardly," Leo said, turning to give his brother a wolfish smile before turning to Danni. "Shall we get the game started?"

"Yes," she said, walking toward the golf cart.

He watched her go, thinking, for the first time since he'd arrived on Nantucket, he was going to have an interesting time.

Danni had deliberately put her name in with Leo's for the golf scramble, but she was a bit surprised and intimidated to be playing with his mother and brother, as well. The Bisset family were pretty much American royalty, and for a small-town girl, being in their presence was a bit heady. But this was the world she aspired to and what she was aiming for in her own life. So, she tucked one of the curls that she'd tried to tame into submission in a low ponytail back behind her ear and lined up her shot.

The golf course was built near the beach, and most of the holes offered a view of the ocean. The sun was shining, and it was a perfect summer day. She knew that Adler had been worried about summer storms ruining the events she and Nick Williams had planned for their destination wedding. But Danni thought the elements were cooperating.

But apparently there were storm clouds gathering between the bride's and groom's families. Nick was the CEO of Williams, Inc. They were Bisset Industries' biggest competition, often going after the same contracts. The rivalry was pretty fierce and frequently made the headlines.

Danni had heard some rumblings at the golf clubhouse before everyone had arrived that there was some scandal brewing about the groom. Something about how August Bisset was actually Nick's father as a result of a secret affair with Cora Williams decades ago.

Had Danni even heard that right? While Adler wasn't related to her uncle by blood, the discovery that Nick was August's son had to put an incredible strain on the wedding couple. Danni hoped that whatever was going on, Nick and Adler could find their way through the crisis.

She teed up her first shot. Everything she knew about golf she'd learned from her dad at the golf course near their home. He was a big one for taking his time and using everything as a teachable moment. Danni had always been impatient, though, and now she was struggling to remember what he'd said. Swing from the hips? Keep her hips steady?

Mainly she just hoped she'd actually hit the ball and, fingers crossed, get it into the hole.

She took a deep breath and held it until she couldn't wait any longer. Then she drew back the club to swing…and missed. Ugh, she was so horrible at sports.

"Want some help?" Leo asked, coming up next to her. "I play regularly so I've gotten pretty good, but before that I was a mess."

She doubted he'd ever been a mess at anything but appreciated him pretending he had been.

"I'd love some tips. My dad said something about my hips—either swing through them or keep them steady…honestly, I can't remember, and the more I concentrate, the worse I'm getting," she admitted.

He smiled. "I know the feeling. Here's the thing—this is just for fun, so relax. I'm not a pro, but I keep my arms straight…like this," he said, moving behind her and adjusting her hands on the club. "When you swing, bring the club back straight and then turn your body in the direction you want the ball to go."

She was trying to concentrate, but honestly, he

was wrapped around her like a big warm hug, and he smelled good. Like one of those luxury stores she and her mom had liked to duck into for a little pretend shopping when Danni was growing up and her parents were working for the public defender's office. She closed her eyes for a second, and it was almost like he was embracing her instead of showing her how to hit the golf ball.

"Got it?" he asked.

She smiled her thanks and then shook her head. She was here to collect intel on a competitor but also maybe pick up some advice, not start falling for his pretty blue eyes, athletic frame and grace. And he was being very generous and kind to her. He'd welcomed her as if they were old friends. Instead of reacting to her catty remark, he'd apologized…to be fair, she definitely thought he owed her one, but it had been sincere, and he'd been very nice since then.

"If I miss again, it's down to user error and nothing to do with your lesson," she said.

"You won't miss," he said. "I'm pretty sure this time you're going to connect and send that ball flying."

She wished she had his confidence.

Wait a second. She *should* have his confidence. It wouldn't hurt. She remembered her grandmother saying that if she thought she couldn't, then she wouldn't.

Danni widened her stance as she'd seen Leo do on

his last putt and then set up her shot. She took a deep breath, and this time, instead of holding it, she kept breathing naturally as she swung. She hit the ball. She was so excited she turned to Leo with a squeal, not even looking where the ball went.

"I hit it!"

"You did. Good job," he said. "You'll be better than me in no time."

She tipped her head to the side. "Let's not get carried away. I think we all know that I'd have to spend most of the next few years on the course every day to get to your level. But I'll settle for at least getting the ball down the green and in the hole."

"I think you'll be able to do that," Leo said. "Are you this determined in every part of your life?"

"I am," she said. "Also, I'm ridiculously stubborn."

"I can see that. I also picked up a bit of temper. I mean, I thought you might hurt the ball if you didn't hit it."

She could see he was teasing her, and she liked it. He was funny, and that was unexpected. She wasn't sure what she'd thought Leo would be like in person. Arrogant and cocky—definitely. But beyond that, she hadn't considered that he'd be so...well, human. "I wouldn't have wanted to maim it."

He threw his head back and laughed, and for a minute Danni forgot she was trying to get business information from him and use him for his connections. She realized that she enjoyed being around him and wanted their time together to continue— something she knew would never happen. They came from two different worlds, and her brief foray into his was just that. Brief.

She needed to remember who she was and why she was here. Men like Leo didn't fall for women like her, and besides, she hadn't come here this weekend for romance. She was here for business.

Leo wasn't on his A game at all. He was a stroke off Logan at each hole and after he'd given Danni some pointers on her swing she was starting to play better. He needed to get his head in the game.

Danni was distracting him.

He finally pulled her aside while his mom and Logan were talking. He wanted to get past this awkwardness, which was totally his fault. Normally his mom would have been the diplomat who put everyone at ease but she was only half paying attention to their foursome and her own golf game.

"You're getting a lot better, but I can still sense some coldness between us. What can I do to make this right?" he asked.

Danni tipped her head to the side, studying him for a moment before narrowing her eyes. "Give me some business advice."

He was surprised by her answer. From what he'd

read and heard, her business was growing quickly. "I'm not sure you need that."

"My dad always says the day you stop learning is the day you die," she quipped. "I could use a mentor."

"Uh."

"Never mind. I forgot I was talking to Leo Bisset. From Fortune Magazine's top 30 under 30."

He watched her as she turned and walked away. Was she serious? Of course she was. He'd sought out mentors and advice the same way when he'd first started out, only he'd had his father and Logan to watch and learn from.

"I see your charm isn't working, as usual," Logan said as he came over to Leo.

He elbowed his brother, intending to ignore him, but Logan dodged the elbow. "She doesn't want to be charmed."

"Oh, ho. So you're going to have to work harder to get her to like you," Logan said. "Not impossible. Even for you."

But Logan was needling him every time they were alone and rubbing in the fact that Leo couldn't get Danni interested in him. He wanted to be chill and act like it didn't matter, but there was a part of him—hell, most of him—that was always competing with Logan and, to a larger extent, their father. Both men had always been charming with everyone and had their pick of women. Even though their dad was married and should say no.

But that wasn't something Leo liked to dwell on. He wanted his father's approval, craved his praise more than he knew was healthy. But that didn't change the fact that he wanted it. He also wasn't a huge fan of the way his father had handled his relationship with Leo's mom over the years. He'd had affairs, which for the most part had been kept quiet—except for the one before Leo's sister, Marielle, was born. Until recently, he'd believed that his parents had worked out all their past troubles.

But the revelations about his father's past cheating, and how Nick Williams was really August Bisset's son, had been hard on their mom, and on the entire family. Imagine everyone's surprise when the mother of the groom turned out to be one of his father's former mistresses. Even worse, they'd had a child together who was about to marry into the Bisset family! It was surreal. The paparazzi were all over the place and gossips sites were hinting that wasn't the end of the story, but Leo hoped in his heart it was.

Logan hated Nick and vice versa, but as for Leo, he was just disappointed that his father, the man he so wanted to be like, was so flawed. It would be hard to ignore the very real possibility that he had those same flaws.

"So…what's the plan?" Logan asked, nodding toward Danni.

Leo glanced at his older brother. Logan looked more like their mom than their dad, with his blond hair and high cheekbones. They both had the same ice-blue eyes. Once Leo had left Bisset Industries to start his own business, they'd begun to get along a lot better. Leo knew it had been down to his constant need to try to beat Logan when they were both working for their father.

"I'm not sure yet," Leo said. He certainly wasn't going to discuss anything with Logan. Danni had asked for business tips and he could do that. That was one area where he didn't have to try hard.

"Sometimes you need a plan."

"I'm not you," Leo pointed out. "I do better when I go off script."

"Are you sure about that?"

Leo shot his brother the bird and then took his club to go and tee off. After they'd all taken their shots, he made sure he was next to Danni as they walked toward the hole.

"Were you serious about wanting me to mentor you?" he asked.

"Yes," she said. "But since we are each other's competition—"

"I don't think you're in my league," he said softly.

"Yet," she said, with a cheeky smile.

"Yet," he agreed. "I'll help you out this weekend. If you do me a favor."

She shrugged and turned to look out at the horizon and the ocean. He gave her the time she needed before she turned back to him, pushing her sunglasses up on her head. She looked so young and earnest, and he had the feeling that whatever she said next was really important to her. And he was scared for her. He'd never been as earnest as she appeared to be.

"What's the favor?"

"Be my 'date' for the weekend. My family is going through some stuff and I could use someone to hang out with away from all that."

"Should you do that? I mean we are talking about a business relationship," she said.

"It's just for the weekend and I've always thought that business isn't personal. It's about competing and winning and producing the best product."

"Okay," she said. But she sounded hesitant.

Which he decided he'd smooth over later.

Two

Danni went into the clubhouse and looked for her assigned table after the golf scramble. They were going to be announcing the winner, and Danni had a hunch that Logan might be it. He'd certainly been the best by one stroke in their group. He and his brother Leo had both played par on most holes and under on a couple.

He'd reluctantly agreed to mentor her in exchange for her being his date. That should assuage her conscience. She still felt a little guilty that she'd used this wedding invitation as a way to broaden her network and was planning to meet as many A-listers as she could to try to expand her business reach and discoverability.

But did she have to feel guilty with Leo? He'd said that business wasn't personal to him. She shook her head and then stopped herself from going down a rabbit hole of dithering. Her assigned table was near the middle of the room, and she started toward it just as Adler Osborn—the bride—noticed her and waved her over.

Adler was radiating a kind of glow that all brides seemed to have, but she also looked tired, and there was an edge to her smile, as if she was trying too hard to be happy. "Hello," Danni greeted her. "How are you hanging in there? According to my mother, she wanted to bolt at least three times the week before her wedding and even more so on the actual day."

Adler laughed and shook her head. "I'm doing okay. There's been a lot of unexpected stuff coming up with family, which I guess is to be expected, given that we are all in one place. How was golf? I see you were teamed up with my aunt and cousins. Were the boys good? Those two like to fight."

"They were funny, actually. They competed the entire time, but they were so sweet with their mom that it was nice to watch. I'm afraid I brought our foursome's score down—or should I say up?"

"Ha. That's okay, it's all in good fun anyway. Your business partner sent over men's and women's bracelets for the wedding guest gift bags, and I can't thank you enough for that. I wasn't expecting it, but it is a nice thing to add."

"I hope you don't mind. We wanted to give everyone something special to remember the day," Danni said. She'd asked Essie to wait until she'd talked to Adler, but apparently she hadn't. "I was going to run it by you first."

"It's fine. I love it. The one you made for my dad is cute—he's going to be over the moon." Adler's father was the rock star Toby Osborn and her mom was Leo's late aunt Musette, who had died when Adler was a baby. "His first hit is so close to his heart, so etching the lyrics on the leather band was clever."

"Well, that song was about you, right?" she asked.

"Yes. It is. So, it's special to me, too," Adler said. "I'm so glad I asked you to do the bridesmaids' gifts. I wanted to make sure that they had a woman's touch, not that Leo isn't fabulous but…well, you have really helped make this wedding special."

"I'm glad, too," Danni said. "And I have really enjoyed working with you. You haven't been…well, like some of my more high-maintenance clients."

"I have tried to not be a bridezilla. Quinn does these high-profile weddings all the time, and she had some stories to tell. I get how easy it would be to drift into that kind of behavior. So much stress to get it all perfect and make sure all the details and events are ideally planned. But mistakes happen. Stuff happens," Adler said.

"Who's Quinn?"

"Oh, she's the producer of the Destination Weddings series, and she's filming this wedding for the show. I don't think you knew her at school but she was one of my roommates."

"No, I didn't know her. And I'm sure everyone in your family would be cool if you were to be a little divaish."

"Ha. My dad likes to be the one owning all the drama," Adler said. "But you're right. I'm so lucky to be doted on by my family. What table are you at for the lunch?"

"Twelve," Danni said. "Somewhere in the middle, I believe."

"Did you bring a plus-one?" Adler asked.

"No. I was going to bring my business partner, but she couldn't make it," Danni said. No use mentioning that they had decided to save money and keep Essie home.

"I'll put you at one of the family tables for dinner tomorrow and for the rehearsal dinner later," Adler said. "My aunt is a good hostess, and you mentioned the boys weren't that bad."

She had to chuckle at how Adler referred to Leo and Logan. They were grown men, older than Adler, and looked nothing like adolescents. "Why do you call them the boys?"

"To keep them in line. They tend to get a little too big for their britches otherwise. They are all successful, good-looking, charming, wealthy…just a little too used to everyone being in awe of them," Adler said.

"I can imagine. Um, actually, Leo asked me to be his 'date' at the rest of these events. I hope that's okay," Danni asked.

"Of course. I'm glad you two are getting along," she said.

Danni was glad she didn't have a chance to respond as Adler motioned for her wedding planner to join them and made arrangements for Danni to be moved to the family tables for the rest of the meals. Then they both went to their tables.

She was surprised when she got to hers and found her nameplate wasn't there. There was a note addressed to her informing her to go to table nine. She looked around, holding the note, and saw Leo waving her over.

She took a deep breath. Leo certainly wasn't one to wait around. And if she were honest she'd admit there was more to the man's appeal than his business acumen. There had been a connection between them, and she couldn't help the little thrill that went through her at the chance of spending more time with him. But she had to make up her mind—either business or pleasure.

And the last thing she wanted to do was lose this opportunity to pick his brain and meet people who could help her move her business forward. She had a history of falling for bad boys who broke her heart, and she was pretty sure Leo fell into that category.

Leo had moved Danni's name card to his table after confirming his brother Logan wasn't staying for the meal. Logan was trying to reconnect with Quinn Murray, his college girlfriend, and Leo was all for his brother taking a break from the family situation. Logan was taking the news that Nick was their half sibling harder than the rest of them. Nick and Logan often went head-to-head in the boardroom, and neither really liked the other.

Logan would figure it out, though. Leo was confident of that. He watched Nick talking to his siblings and parents toward the front of the room. It wasn't too hard to see a resemblance to their family...to their father. Nick had dark hair and dark brown eyes like August. He also had the height, but then, his stepfather, Tad, was also tall. Apparently everyone in the Williams family had already known that Nick wasn't Tad's son, but none of them, including Tad, had known that August was the father until yesterday afternoon, when Nick's mom and August had seen each other for the first time in decades.

News that Nick was really August's son had thrown everyone for a loop. Poor Adler, who'd wanted a scandal-free wedding, was upset, as she had a right to be. But for once the scandal wasn't coming from her rock star father, the legendary Toby

Osborn, and the drama his sexcapades with multiple younger partners had always caused.

Leo knew that Adler, with help from his mother, would sort everything out. He was more curious about this newly discovered half brother. His family dynamic with his siblings was already highly competitive and close-knit. How would Nick mix in with them? For now it seemed like he wasn't sure he wanted to. Nick ran his family business and from all reports was following in Tad Williams's footsteps. As far as any of them knew, Nick might never want to be part of the Bisset family. He was thirty-six, so finding out he had more siblings at this stage might not be something he wanted to deal with.

Leo took a moment to make sure that Danni's name card was at the place setting next to his and then walked over to Nick, where he stood with two of his brothers. One of them looked like trouble and the other had an easy smile and held his hand out to Leo as he approached.

"Noah Williams," he said. "You're Leo, right?"

"I am," Leo said, shaking his hand. "Nick, Asher, good to see you both again. How'd you do on the links?"

The conversation was easygoing as the men discussed the golf game from the morning. But it felt weird, and Leo knew he wasn't the only one who noticed it.

"Just trying to figure out this new brother thing,"

he said when an awkward silence built. "Figured we should at least try to be friendly."

"I agree," Noah said. "You live on Long Island, right?"

"I do," he said.

"Me, too. I'm doing the acting thing part-time, but I'll be home all summer," he said, pausing for effect. "I'm having a killer masquerade party beginning of August. I'd love it if you'd come. Nick and Adler will be back from their honeymoon, so it will be a fun blowout."

"Sounds like my kind of party," Leo said. "Do you have my details?"

They exchanged numbers before the wedding planner came to tell them to take their seats. Leo left the exchange feeling…not sure how he felt. His father had thrown a wrench into their entire family dynamic decades earlier when he'd had an affair with Cora Williams, who'd gone by the name of Bonnie Smith back then. The affair had ended when she'd realized she was pregnant and she'd never told August. She'd kept his name a secret when she married Tad Williams because of his rivalry with Bisset Industries. Now, they were all trying to figure out how to deal with this bond that none of them really wanted but couldn't ignore.

He went back to his table and noticed that his mom's seat was empty. He hoped she was okay. As much as he admired his dad for his business acumen, he hated the way he'd hurt Leo's mom again and again. Cora…had Cora been his first affair? Was his mom wondering that now? Finding out that August had cheated on her when she'd been pregnant with his brother Logan had been a blow.

Leo shook his head as one of his uncles came over to the table. Time to put on a game face and make sure that everyone had a good time at Adler's party. He didn't want his father's mistake to hurt his cousin any more than it already had.

He noticed Adler was talking to Danni and wondered what they were talking about. Probably none of his business, he thought, chagrined. She'd sort of surprised him. The bracelet she wore was high-quality, but it would be hard to judge her and her business without seeing more of her product. He could do that later, he thought as she glanced around, looking for her table.

He waved at her and watched as she tucked the note that he'd left at her table into her pocket and walked toward him. She moved like a woman with purpose. She had an easy smile, and he saw how people readily returned it. She was the kind of person who could do well in the world of influencers. Should he help her out? Give her a hand in growing her business?

He thought about it a bit more but got distracted by the way the sunlight was making her thick, curly hair seem more alive than it had outside. He realized that she looked like one of those fairy-tale princesses from the books Mari used to ask him to read her at night. Danni had a heart-shaped face, a cute little nose and a mouth that made him think of kissing her.

Awkward.

She'd asked him to be her mentor. And he had said he'd do it for this weekend. Which meant he needed to check his libido and do the right thing. He knew in his gut that his father...well, that he didn't want to be the kind of womanizer his father had been.

All of which just added to the dilemma of whether he should have offered his help as her mentor. He had meant it when he said business wasn't personal, but if he started to be personal with her, then it would change the dynamic.

He'd been burned by that very thing. But he told himself that this time he was going into it with his eyes open. And he didn't know if he could handle another dicey relationship right now.

Leo kept the conversation at the table moving throughout the lunch, which was impressive, given that they were mixed in with his older relatives as well as his ten-year-old cousin, Jen, who wanted him to take her on his next photo shoot in Bermuda. Leo was so easygoing about his famous friends, and his jet-set lifestyle added another dimension to the man Danni was coming to know. She turned to Jen.

"Are you doing anything fun this summer?" she asked.

"Just the wedding, and then we'll be at the cottage for the rest of July and August. Then it's back to school."

"Where do you go to school? On Nantucket?" Danni asked.

Jen tucked her black hair behind her ear. "St. Francis in Boston. We live in Boston. I was supposed to go to a boarding school next year, but I didn't want to, and my mom said that it was time to make some new Bisset traditions."

"Good for her. And good for you for standing up for yourself. It's hard to tell your parents what you want to do," Danni said.

"It is," Jen agreed. "It must be nice to be a grownup and do your own thing."

"It is," Danni said. She didn't want to tell Jen that parents still could influence your life after you were an adult. Her parents were keeping up the pressure for her to rejoin the family law firm, which they'd started when her siblings were in high school, but she didn't want to.

Everyone had expected her to practice law, and she'd done it. Followed the family path and gone into practice with them. But to be honest it had been killing her soul.

One of the hardest conversations she'd ever had with her parents was when she told them she wanted to start her own business. They'd been supportive, and it had taken her a while to realize that they expected her to get bored with it and return to the law firm.

Her dream was to have her own business. Nothing as big and far-reaching as Bisset Industries, but her own little shop…which was why she should be picking Leo's brain at this lunch instead of talking with his cute little second cousin.

Danni knew she didn't have that killer instinct, and a part of her wanted to believe that good girls could go just as far in business. But there were times when she wondered if she was just kidding herself.

"Leo, how's your mom handling everything that's come out about—"

"We're not talking about that during Adler's wedding, Uncle Joe," Leo said.

Joe nodded and then shook his head. "Sorry to have brought it up. Your mom is a class act."

"She is. Some say that I inherited her charm. What do you think, Jen?" he asked his little cousin seated next to her.

She laughed. "You're silly."

"Hmm…not the image I want to project around Danni."

"Too late," Danni quipped, happy to help change the subject. "This key lime pie is good."

The discussion turned to the food and slowly everyone left the table until it was just the two of them.

The lunch ended before Danni had a chance to ask Leo anything that would help her business. Though a part of her was curious about whatever was going on with his family, she had to focus on this mentorship. She'd had a few different questions in the back of her mind, but it was hard to transition from "pass the bread basket" to "how did you find a reliable production factory?"

"That was fun," Leo said. "I always forget how Uncle Luca is like a totally relaxed version of my dad. He's so much easier to just talk to."

"I don't know your dad at all. Is he intense?"

"Oh, yeah, like Logan and me dialed up to eleven," Leo said. "He always owns whatever room he walks into."

"That can't be true. I didn't even notice him today," Danni said, wondering about Leo's relationship with his father. She'd read in his bio about his family, and of course everyone—well, maybe not everyone, but most people—had heard of the Bisset family. They were like the Kennedys but without all the tragedy. They were a big, wealthy family that had connections everywhere in all branches of society. Business, politics, the arts. But she hadn't read much on August Bisset—her focus was on Leo.

"He's not here," Leo said with a dry laugh. "Trust me, when you do meet him, you'll know what I'm talking about."

"I'll take your word for it. I guess we're free this

afternoon until the rehearsal dinner," Danni said. "Are you in the wedding party?"

"No," Leo said, shaking his head. "I'm taking some photos of Adler for our family, but otherwise I'm not really involved. I think Adler wanted to keep my branch as far away from Nick's family as she could."

"Yeah? I heard there was a bit of a rivalry, but surely it's not that bad," Danni said. She had heard the rumors of the rivalry, and the family businesses were often mentioned in the news for edging each other in some big deal or another. But she always thought it was media hype; she didn't think big feuds like that existed anymore. But she was the first to admit that she might be naive.

"It's bad, all right. I mean, Dad almost didn't come to the wedding, and Adler is my mom's only niece on her side of the family. Mom helped raise Adler when she was younger," Leo said.

"Wow."

"I know, crazy, right? That's the Bisset family. What are you doing this afternoon?" he asked.

She thought about it for a minute and realized this might be a good time to pick his brain. "I'm going to try to take some photos to use for my social media accounts. Got any tips?"

"What kind of tips?" he asked.

"Your pictures on Instagram are so…great. I mean, it's more than a filter, it's how you set them up and everything. I could spend hours looking at them. I've tried to analyze why, but I can't put my finger on it." She waited to see if he would be offended that she'd asked, but instead he rubbed the back of his neck and then pulled his phone from his pocket.

"I don't know if I can tell you why you like the pictures, but what I do is try to capture not the product I'm selling but more of a feeling I want to evoke. So, your bracelet isn't the focus but instead that bottle of Veuve Clicquot in the background and the flowers, and then you reaching for the glass. Try it," he said.

She leaned over and reached for the champagne flute as he'd directed her.

"Wait. Adjust your bracelet so the charm is dangling in front of the bottle," he said, then reached over and moved the bracelet and then stepped back again and snapped the picture.

"What do you think?" he asked, inviting her closer to look at his phone. She leaned over to look down and realized that he'd captured something more than her bracelet, and for the first time when she looked at her product, she saw a hint of a different lifestyle.

"I like it," she said, looking up at him, and their eyes met.

"I do, too," he said, not looking at the phone but at her. She shivered as she felt that current go through her again, and she quickly looked away.

She took a deep breath and looked back at him.

She realized how close he was, close enough to really appreciate the flecks of gold in his eyes. She hadn't let herself dwell too much on the fact that he was a very good-looking man.

She was noticing it now.

And it wasn't too long before he noticed her noticing. He lifted his hand and tucked a curly strand of hair that had fallen to lie against her cheek back behind her ear.

She shivered again and stepped away. *Focus, Danni.* Otherwise she'd be back in the law firm when the summer was over.

Three

Leo got the text summoning him to a family meeting at his gran's house and almost ditched it to stay with Danni. But given what had been happening at family meetings lately he knew he couldn't. Reluctantly he said goodbye to Danni and headed up to the cottage. Since he'd arrived on Nantucket, every family meeting had led to a new scandal. He wasn't naive enough to believe that this time would be any different.

Gran's butler, Michael, let Leo in and led him to the back of the house. His sister, Marielle, was seated alone in the sunroom when he arrived. She smiled over at him. "I bet everyone is having flashbacks to the texts we used to get to discuss the *M* problem," she said with a wink.

For the last few years, Marielle had been the most outrageous thing about the family, after her high-profile affair with a married Formula One driver, but that had all ended when the driver had been killed in a crash and Marielle had retreated from the spotlight to try to change her life. She'd managed to do that and six months earlier had fallen in love with Inigo Velasquez, another Formula One driver. One who loved her back this time.

"I kind of like that there isn't an *M* problem anymore," Leo said, going over to hug his sister and then sit next to her on the love seat.

"Me, too. How's business? Logan mentioned you had another jewelry designer–slash–social media influencer in your group at golf," Marielle said.

He could tell she was fishing for information about Danni. "Is that all he said?"

"Nah, he let slip you'd insulted her in a press interview and were trying to get back in her good graces," Marielle said with a laugh. "Who is she?"

"Danni Eldridge. She's not an influencer—well, not really. She has a small business designing bracelets and watchbands. She did the jewelry for Adler's bridesmaids, I gather. And yes, she did come up in an interview I did a while back. I said she was trying to ride my coattails."

"You really have a way with words. No wonder people think the Bissets are arrogant."

He shrugged. "To be fair, a lot of Etsy shops have copied my font and storefront images. One of them was even illegally using my photos to sell their cheap products."

"Fair enough. So what's the deal with Danni? Did she do that?" Marielle asked.

"No, she has too much pride in her own products to do that. The deal… I like her. She's cute and funny. I didn't really know who she was when I was asked about her. I just lumped her in with everyone else."

"Do you wish you hadn't said it?"

"About her? Maybe. I mean, I stand by what I said about my competitors in general, though. It's hard to do what I've done. A lot of people assume Dad or Logan gave me the money to start my business and that I'm just the face of the company. But I work hard—"

"I know you do," Marielle said.

"Hi, all. Where are Mom and Dad? Isn't this meeting supposed to be starting soon?" Leo's brother Zac asked as he came in.

"I don't know," Marielle said. "Michael told me to wait in here. Gran's coming as well, but she had a Pilates session just wrapping up, so we're waiting for her."

Leo wasn't surprised that his maternal grandmother was going to be here. Normally, she stayed away from Bisset business but she'd been playing hostess to the family this weekend. After the news that their father had had a child with another woman, their mom had been subdued and not herself. She was a strong woman, but this kind of news was hard to hear. Gran would want to show up to support her daughter.

"I'm here. What did I miss?" Logan asked as he came into the room.

"Nothing. So far it's just us," Leo said.

"Just us?" Dare asked, coming in.

"Yeah. It's been a while since we've all been together," Leo said. "This is nice. Are you thinking of staying in this part of the world, Zac?"

"I wish. I've got to get back to training for the America's Cup," Zac said. "But I hope to make more trips this way in the future."

"I'm glad to hear that," Leo's mother said, joining them.

She seemed to have aged by about ten years overnight. Normally she looked at least twenty years younger than sixty, but not today. Leo got up and went over to give her a hug and noticed his brothers and sister had the same idea. They were all in a big group hug around their mom, and she hugged them all back the way she had when they were little. But Leo heard her draw a ragged breath, and then she started to cry.

"Kiddos. This new thing…it's my fault. I don't know how to tell you—"

"Don't do it, yet," Leo's father said as he arrived. "Carlton is on his way. We can discuss it when he is here."

Carlton was his father's press relations guy and had been spinning the Bisset family scandals since before Leo was born.

As she took a deep breath, Carlton burst through the door, with Gran following close behind but at a slower pace.

"Are we all here?" the family adviser asked in the brisk, no-nonsense tone he used when handling any PR problem. "Because there are new developments."

Once the entire family, including Gran, were in the sun room, Carlton read them a newswire story about a nurse from a small rural hospital who claimed that Nick wasn't the only baby Bonnie Smith aka Cora Williams had delivered that night. In fact, she'd had twins and had given one to Juliette Bisset to raise after her pregnancy ended in a stillbirth.

Leo almost couldn't comprehend what he heard. Mari went stock-still next to him, and he put his arm around her as he turned to his mother.

His father had stood up. "Jules, how is this possible? Nick and Logan don't look like each other. Is it true?"

One look at his mother's face confirmed it. She took a deep breath and wrapped her arms around herself as she stood there next to the floor-to-ceiling bookcases.

She recounted the story of her going into labor. Auggie had been away on a business trip.

"Skip to the part where you swap your dead baby for me," Logan said.

Leo gasped and started to lunge for his brother but Mari stopped him and he let her. Logan's face was a cold mask and Leo realized that his brother was having a difficult time hearing all of this.

"Don't be such a dick," Leo said.

"I'll be whatever I want, she's not my mom," Logan said. "Right? That's true, isn't it?"

August cursed and turned on him, but when their eyes met, Logan knew his father understood his anguish. His dad started toward him, but he just shook his head.

"Finish the story," Logan said curtly.

"My birth was quicker, and I was in the recovery room," Juliette said. "I was crying when Bonnie— I mean Cora—came back in. She was crying, too. She had anticipated having one child but two was too many for her to handle. She'd gotten a partial scholarship to go back to school and thought she could manage with one child but with two she was going to have to skip college.

"I told her that my marriage would probably be over when my husband learned about the stillborn baby. The pregnancy had brought us back together.

But I knew without that baby, your father and I would struggle to stay together."

"That's not—"

"Don't say it's not the truth, Auggie. We both know that we were barely keeping ourselves together as a couple then. Bonnie said she was going to have to give up one of the babies or maybe it would be better if she gave them both up," Juliette said.

"So you offered to raise one as our son," August said.

"I did. I also gave her money to support herself and get some help for the son she kept," Juliette said. "We swapped the bracelets and Logan became my son. I nursed you, you became my baby at that moment. I never thought of you as anything other than my son."

"So how did the nurse know?" Logan asked.

"She knew my son was stillborn and had gone away to do the paperwork. Even though Bonnie and I told her that she was mistaken, she knew the truth. I offered her a bribe, which she was reluctant to take but then Bonnie—I mean Cora—said that no one would ever find out, there were only the three of us. This way the boys would both be raised by mothers who could afford them and who wanted them. The doctor had already signed the paperwork and it was simply down to us filling it in. Bonnie took it from her and signed it. I thought that was it."

"You should have brought this to me," August said. "I could have—"

"What? What would you have done?" his mom demanded.

Logan got up and stormed out of the room, Leo started to follow but Dare stopped him. "Let him alone."

Leo did, but he felt his family was falling apart. He wanted to comfort his mom, punch his dad and maybe have it out with someone.

"Did you meet him? Was he as douchey in person as we thought he'd be?" Essie Palmer asked Danni while they were video chatting. Her friend and business partner had a way of getting right to the point.

Danni was sitting on the porch of her family's cottage as she tried to figure out her next move at the wedding. "Actually, he was really nice. And Adler loves the jewelry we gifted her…"

"Did she mind if we use her name in our advertising?"

Danni hadn't had the courage to ask Adler about that yet. She nodded, but her friend must have seen the hesitation in her expression.

Essie raised both eyebrows and shook her head. "Don't even say anything. You didn't ask because you don't want to impose."

"You're right," Danni admitted.

"I know how hard it is for you to use your connections, but you want this to be your job. You have to be more ruthless."

"I know, you're right. Leo and I were talking today about how there's nothing personal about business. But it feels personal to me, especially when I'm dealing with people I like."

"No," Essie said on a laugh. "That's why you're holding yourself back. Business is business."

"I don't know what that means," she said. "But Leo did help me stage a photo. I'm sending it to you now. I want to use it on our social media. What do you think?"

She texted the photo to Essie and noticed on her camera roll that there was a photo of Leo that she hadn't meant to take. He was handsome, and there was something about him that made her think very personal thoughts. Not business at all.

"Damn. He's good. He just took this photo for you?" Essie asked.

"Yeah. I mean, I did ask for some tips, and he set this up. It looks, well, more professional than my usual shots. I want to make sure our shop links for the bracelet are updated, and then I'm going to post it."

"I'll update the links as soon as we're off the call and text you when I'm done," Essie said. "I'm proud of you asking him for help."

"I figured that it was okay. He knows that we're

in the same business, and he could just say no to me. I mean, it's not like we are friends or anything"

"Anything?"

Why had she said that to Essie? Her friend was way too observant, and Danni had the hots for Leo. He had a magnetic personality that had drawn her in despite her many misgivings. And there had been that tingle that she was still trying to convince herself she had imagined.

"Just saying," she said.

"Okay. He is cute. I wouldn't blame you if there was something more," Essie said.

"I would. I want to keep my distance, you know. He's a rival. I want to be good enough that he sees me as competition, not some woman he met at a wedding."

"Why can't you be both?" Essie asked. "You are too quick to put someone in one box and leave them there."

"I don't even know what you're talking about."

"Stan. Mark. Jesse."

"They are business contacts and partners, Ess. They have never been anything else and they don't want to be anything else," Danni said, but she knew her friend was right. She'd turned down all three of them when they'd asked her out. Stan was a corporate vice president for a luxury hotel chain that she'd been trying to get to carry her jewelry in its boutiques.

Mark ran the warehouse they used for their inventory, and Jesse…well, he was just a flirt.

"Leo isn't a business partner, and you could just have fun with him this weekend and then still use the connection when you get home. Not every guy has to be a serious relationship," Essie said.

"I know," she said, but in her heart, she wasn't that casual about it. She wasn't interested in hooking up with anyone just for fun at this time when she was trying to get her business off the ground and stand on her own. She didn't want Leo to have the impression that she'd used him. Or for anyone else to think that. This was her thing and she wanted to earn it.

"Okay. Enough of the lecture. I think you should try to get more photos like this one that Leo helped you with," Essie said.

They discussed staging some more photos and a media plan for the weekend. Together they created a list of images that Danni should try to capture before they hung up.

Danni stretched her legs, propping them up on the railing as she scrolled through her photos. The best were the ones that Leo had taken, but she found herself staring at the off-center photo of Leo.

His face was serious. He was staring at a point beyond the camera; she knew it was the champagne bottle, but it was almost too easy to imagine he'd been looking at her. Had he felt the same zing she had?

Honestly, he wasn't the kind of man who'd feel

a zing with a woman like her. It wasn't an insult to herself; she was too low-key for a man like Leo. She knew that to boost her profile she should change her energy and her attitude and be more hard-driving. But she wasn't ready to let go of that part of herself, even to be successful. And maybe that was what Essie had been getting at. She needed to become a different woman to have the success she wanted.

But the kind of woman who would have an affair with Leo Bisset?

"Affair" was such an old-fashioned term but the truth was she did want an affair with him. She had felt a connection when he'd touched her, but this was her last chance to make a go of her small business. She couldn't—wouldn't—risk it for an affair with Leo Bisset.

He was a playboy and a flirt and she wasn't going to put herself on the line with him.

Leo was angry and hurt. He hadn't expected to react so strongly to the announcement that Logan wasn't his mother's child.

He still couldn't believe what his mother had told them. For once even Carlton had little to say. Why hadn't they discovered all this sooner? It was true that Cora had gone by a different name back then, and she'd married Tad Williams much later. The Bissets didn't realize Cora—aka Bonnie Smith—was Tad Williams's wife until they all met her the other day when they arrived for Adler's wedding. The Bissets and Williamses were enemies; they'd always avoided each other socially. It was bad enough that Juliette's niece was marrying Nick Williams.

Also, Nick and Logan weren't identical; in fact, Logan was often told he looked like Juliette Bisset, though it now turned out they weren't even related by blood.

Leo's brother had experienced a double blow. First, that his father's affair with Cora made his adversary Nick Williams his brother. And now that he, too, was the other woman's son and Nick was his twin!

Now the rest of the family sat in shocked silence. Even though Leo acknowledged that his mother had done wrong, he knew where the blame lay, and it wasn't with her. It was with his dad. August had always been so determined to take what he wanted that he never thought of the consequences.

"Dad, you never think of the consequences of your actions," Leo said. "You had an affair and then moved on and disappeared when Mom was about to give birth. I've always wanted your approval and to be just like you but now I'm glad I'm not."

There was a murmur from Leo's siblings.

"That's a little bit harsh," Dare said.

His eldest brother was used to being the voice of reason in their family and in his job as a politician. But Leo knew there was no denying it.

"Is it, Dad?" Leo asked their father.

Even Marielle was watching August, all of them waiting to hear what he had to say. Their father had lorded over them all for their entire lives, and now chinks were starting to appear in his armor. Leo admitted to himself that they had always been there but for the most part they had ignored it.

"No. It's not unfair to say. I was very determined to build an empire out of Bisset Industries. Your uncle and aunt weren't interested in running the business, and I knew if I wanted it to last for more than one generation, I was going to need kids to pass it on to. I wanted another son, because Dare wouldn't be enough."

"Thanks, Dad," Dare said, reaching into his pocket and pulling out a pack of cigarettes that was at least ten years old and looked worn from being carried around for too long. He looked at the pack and then cursed and shoved it back in his pocket. "You never do mince words. So you would have left Mom if she'd lost the baby… I mean, if you knew she'd lost it?"

August shoved both hands through his hair and then turned his back on them. He put his hands on his hips and bowed his head but didn't answer Dare. He didn't have to, Leo thought. They all knew the truth.

"Dad?" Marielle asked. "That's not true, is it? You love Mom."

August turned to Marielle, who got up and went

over to him. Those two had always been close, but now Leo could tell that his sister was seeing their dad through different eyes. Probably the same way he was. His entire life Leo had wanted to be like August Bisset, and now…well, now he wasn't sure. He didn't want to be the kind of man who kept his family in line through bullying and intimidation, Leo thought. The same went for August's staff—he treated them the same way.

"I do love your mom, Mari. But it's taken a lifetime for me to realize that I didn't want to lose her. I'm not entirely sure what I would have done if I'd known about the stillbirth," he said.

Leo shook his head and walked out of the room and out of his grandmother's house. He didn't want to hear anything else his father had to say. Their relationship had always been too strained, and his mom had said it was because they were so alike. Something that Leo had used to fuel his ambition and keep himself moving toward a new goal. Never standing still, never being satisfied with the success he'd found.

But that was all confusing now. Was that the man he was destined to become? Was he going to be laying waste to everything he'd built someday because he'd never taken the time to appreciate what he had?

He didn't know. It was too much to delve into at the moment. He stepped out into the summer heat and looked at the driveway full of expensive cars.

They all had to acknowledge the effect of being a Bisset and seeing the example that August and their mom had set for them. They were all overachievers who would stop at nothing to get ahead. For Marielle it had been an affair with a married man. For himself it had been ruthlessly stepping over his acquaintances and building his empire from the ground up. But was it time to step away from that model?

Hell, he knew it was. But he had no idea how else to operate. How else to build his business and his life.

He ignored his car and walked toward the town center instead. It was busy, since the summer season meant everyone was headed to the beach. But Leo just put on his sunglasses and ignored the families and tourists all seeming to enjoy this paradise of an island.

Nantucket that had been their sanctuary since they were kids…maybe because they'd always come to visit with their mom and August had stayed in the city working all summer. Again, Leo felt like he'd been punched in the gut, and his heart was broken in a way. He wondered how Logan was handling this.

His brother had always been the best of both their mom and their dad, and now Logan was going to have to deal with the fact that he wasn't part Wallis—their mother's maiden name—as he'd always believed. But something else. Someone else.

Leo knew it was going to be a long time before his brother could forgive his parents for that.

"Leo?"

He looked over and noticed Danni was sitting on the porch of one of the smaller cottages close to the main street. She stood up as she saw him and waved.

He waved back. He didn't dwell on it but realized he'd felt so lost until he saw her. She wasn't his salvation or anything like that, but she was a distraction…and he desperately needed one.

Four

Danni's half-formed plan of asking Leo to mentor her seemed to be getting a nudge from the universe, she thought as he opened the white picket fence gate and walked up to the porch.

"Just chilling?" he asked.

He seemed tense, even though he was being cordial and friendly. There was an energy around him that made her feel like he was on edge. She knew that weddings stirred up all kinds of emotions in people. In her experience it was mainly women, but she realized that was a bit sexist.

"Yeah. Want to join me?" she asked.

"Yes. But I can't sit still right now. Could I interest you in a walk or bike ride?" he asked.

"A walk is right up my alley. Let me grab my hat and I'll be right with you," she said.

She dashed into the cottage and changed her flip-flops for some Keds and put on a wide-brimmed straw hat that she'd had for years. She took a quick look in the mirror, hoping her outfit was cute, but with her curly hair responding to the humidity, she looked like...well, like Hermione Granger when she didn't use a spell to tame her hair. She tossed the hat on the bench since it wasn't sitting on her hair very well and grabbed a baseball cap that had Nantucket embroidered on it. She forced her hair into a ponytail that she anchored with the hat's Velcro strap at the back.

She stepped outside and noticed that Leo was texting, his fingers moving at a furious pace. She pulled her phone out and checked to see if there was anything in the WhatsApp wedding group. But there wasn't any news. She wondered if he was dealing with business. Or maybe it was personal, she thought, and immediately stopped herself. Because it was still dangerous to even think about mixing business and pleasure with this man.

"Have you been down to the beach yet? I have a favorite spot for looking at shells. It's a bit off the beaten path, but I think you might like it," she said. Internally she wanted to shake her head. She sounded like she was a tour guide instead of a professional businesswoman. She was struggling to find the balance between getting what she wanted from him and being friendly. She'd give anything for an ounce of Essie's boldness, but she knew she wasn't going to be able to magically gain that.

"Sounds great. I really don't want to be around crowds right now," he said.

"I get that. I bet you have fans—do you call them fans? Followers?—that recognize you everywhere you go," she said.

He smiled over at her. "I do, but that's not an issue. I love talking to them and posing for photos. Without them I'd be just another trust-fund guy who struck out on his own to try to prove there's more to him than his family's legacy. Or maybe I'm just trying to fill up my time."

She led the way down the path and onto the sidewalk. He fell into step beside her, and she wondered if he wanted to talk. She thought he had something on his mind. People often told her she was a good listener.

"Everything okay with your family? I didn't see your mom after our golf round," Danni said.

"She's oaky. Something from the past… Actually, she's not okay. Our family is having a bit of a crisis. Not exactly what you wanted to hear, right?" he asked.

Danni stopped walking and reached out to take

his hand and hold it. A tingle went up her arm, but she shoved that reaction to the back of her mind. "I don't want to hear it because I like your family and want them to be okay. But if you need to talk, I'm here. Just tell me what you need."

"Why?" he asked suddenly. "Why are you being so nice?"

"You did me a solid favor earlier. It was nothing to you and everything to me," she admitted. "I owe you."

"That was business," he said with a wink. "This is…a hot mess. I mean, it's so crazy I wouldn't even know where to start."

"Then just say whatever you want to. I'll be honest, I don't know much about your family. Your dad seems a bit larger than life. Logan, obviously, is following in his footsteps, and from what I read, you are, too—"

"That's part of it. I always wanted to be bigger and bolder than Dad, but now…I'm not sure," Leo said.

"I get that," Danni said. "I mean, not on as big a scale as your family. But my entire family are lawyers. Parents and two older siblings. And I want something else. It makes every family get-together so…tense."

Leo looked over at her. "Did you ever want to be just like your mom or dad?"

She shook her head. "Not really. I mean, I wanted their approval, so I went to the schools they wanted me to and took the classes they urged me to take. I even went to law school and passed the bar and practiced for a year. But it just felt like it wasn't me."

Leo turned to face her. "Well, I have always felt like I was just like my father. That I would have been his heir apparent if I'd been born first, and I wanted nothing more than to make him see that in me."

"I think we all grow up wanting to be like our parents. They're always sort of our first heroes."

"You think so?"

She shrugged. Why else would she have gone to law school? The ultimatum they'd given her, the condescension she'd felt when she'd stood her ground and insisted she was going to make her small business work had shown her a different side of her parents. "For me. But it's hard when you realize they have feet of clay."

"Yeah, well, today... I learned some things about my dad that are making me question everything about him and about myself, and I'm not really sure where to go from here."

She had no advice to give him, and really, the pain in his voice when he talked about his father made her realize that this was more complex than she had thought. She turned so that they were facing each other on the sidewalk. At least with her folks they still had a solid relationship.

"Well, let's start with the walk on the beach, okay?"

* * *

Leo realized there was something very sweet about Danni, which made the cynical part of him acknowledge she was probably never really going to be good in a high-stress, cutthroat business world, which the world of influencers was. He wasn't an influencer himself, though he used influencers to promote his brand and his sister was one. But he knew that it was very hard to succeed in that field. Despite the fact that Danni was trying to sell her own products, she'd need to grow her audience enough to make that crossover from Etsy shop to her own brick-and-mortar store. And looking down at her heart-shaped face after she'd just been so kind and sweet, he didn't see her making it.

He reached out to brush a stubborn curl back behind her ear under the baseball cap, and it immediately sprang back to wrap around his finger. He liked her hair. He liked her face and her mouth, which looked perfect for kissing. Normally he didn't size up mouths, but there was something about Danni and her lips that kept drawing his eyes and his thoughts to them. She had some sort of light pink gloss on her lips, and of course she had an easy smile that made him want to smile, too.

Despite all the tension, anger and hurt that he felt at this moment, she was making him want to smile. That was saying something. He saw how that was her real strength. And maybe that was what had appealed to him about her bracelet—something about the design reflected her innate kindness. He wasn't sure how a piece of jewelry could convey that, but hers had.

"You're staring at me, aren't you?" she asked. "Has my hair escaped the hat?"

"I am looking at you," he said, bringing his hand up to rub his thumb lightly along her jaw. "I'm thinking about kissing you, Danni. What do you think about that?"

The days of a guy stealing a kiss were long gone, and he had to admit there were times when he missed them, but at the same time, he sincerely hoped all the girls he'd kissed in high school and in college hadn't felt like he was pushing himself on them or taking something they hadn't wanted to give.

"I wouldn't mind," she admitted. "I've been thinking the same thing."

"You have? That's always a good sign," he replied. He slid his hands along the sides of her neck, noticing the small birthmark behind her ear, then down to her shoulders as he leaned in the slightest bit. She tipped her head more to the side and took a breath.

He leaned down and then hesitated. He wasn't in the best place to start anything right now. He was angry at his father, unsure of the man he wanted to be. Kissing Danni was a distraction, and he wasn't going to pretend it was more than that. But she was kind and sweet, and what if this meant more to her?

"It's just a kiss," she said wryly. "I mean, I can see that you probably think I'm going to be immediately starting my dream wedding wish list at retailers, but honestly, I don't know you. You're hot and everything, but that's all."

He took a step back and started laughing. "God, I'm sorry, Danni. I am just off my game today, or maybe just with you. I hope to have that kiss later. But I think you hit the nail on the head with that comment, and it's made me realize I really don't know you."

"You don't? Just kidding, of course you don't. I had an idea of what you'd be like, and let me say that it totally missed the mark. You are so not what I was expecting," she said.

He took her hand in his and started walking again. "Tell me something about you. Let's get to know each other."

She nibbled on her bottom lip, and he felt that sizzle of arousal go through him again, but he liked it. Finally, he felt something that was exciting and new.

"Okay. But I feel like I should warn you, I do want your advice for my business. So, I'm going to pick your brain for that, too."

He stopped and looked over at her. "I honestly won't be upset by anything business-related between us. I swear."

"Okay. I just don't want to use you," she said.

And those were words he'd never uttered himself

or heard his father say. Every person they met was either someone who could bring them closer to achieving success or not worth their time. He realized that he'd probably missed out on a lot of friendships in his life by following in his father's footsteps. Maybe it was time to try things Danni's way.

"Gaining knowledge and using it to your advantage isn't using me. I won't let you use me if you don't let me use you," he said.

"Deal."

"Kiss on it?" he asked. His hesitation from a moment earlier had already gone up in smoke.

"Not yet. Not until you tell me something that your fan base doesn't know. Who is the real Leo Bisset?"

Before today, he would have answered that he was pretty much what the world saw on social media, but he knew that wasn't true. "Let's see…well, I hate wearing deck shoes. I mean, I know I have a brand partnership with Sperry, and we collaborated on a line. I endorse them, and I do wear the shoes all the time, but if I wasn't in a partnership, I'd wear a pair of ratty old canvas shoes that I keep at my gran's."

"That is shocking," she said with a wink. "Are they comfortable?"

"Yes. So it's not that. They make me feel like I'm working, and the ratty ones I could never photograph or wear when I was going to an event," he said.

"I like that you have them."

"Why?"

"It makes you seem more real," she said softy.

"Do I come across as fake?"

"Well…" She wrinkled her nose and then gave an awkward little laugh.

"So yes. Why?"

"Um, I asked you to tell me something real and you talked about shoes," she said.

"What more can I do to show you I'm real?" he asked, realizing that he wanted to impress her. Which was odd for him.

"Why did you strike out on your own? Not the standard answer you gave me earlier but in your gut, what made you do it?" she asked.

"Wow, that's getting very personal."

She shrugged again, that delicate little movement of her shoulders. "You're the one who wanted a kiss and I don't kiss strangers."

Had he ever worked this hard for a kiss? No. And maybe that was why he craved one from her.

"Okay, well then." He took a deep breath. He didn't think he'd ever told another human being this. "I wanted to see if I was like my Bisset ancestors who built a dynasty out of nothing. I could have taken a senior role and proven myself to my family but I needed to prove myself to me."

He arched one eyebrow at her and cocked his head to the side. "That personal enough?"

"It'll do."

"Now what about you?"

What about her?

She wished there were some easy answer that she could give that would make her seem cute and clever, but the truth was she'd never had a filter, and she wanted to blurt out all the things that most people never noticed about her. Instead she contented herself with channeling Essie. What would Essie say?

"I think most people underestimate me," she said, speaking from the heart. "They mistake kindness for being a pushover, and then are surprised when I'm not. I'm also ridiculously competitive."

"You are? I didn't see that today on the golf course," he said.

"Not that way. More with myself. Like if I see something that I think I can achieve, like being a successful small-business owner, then I don't let anything stand in my way. I've been told that I'm competitive in the courtroom, too."

"Are you? Do you want to go back to practicing?"

"No."

He laughed at the way she said it so quickly and forcefully. "Why not?"

"I'm good at it but it's not my passion. My parents' passion is law, so they don't really get it. They've given me time off to try and make my business work and if I don't by the end of the year, I have to go back. But I won't let myself fail."

He laughed in that way of his that made her smile. "I'm the same way. It's not about the other people in my industry—it's about the next mountain that I want to climb. I'm looking ahead, not to my left or right."

She liked that. "So that's what you meant when you said you don't really see business as being personal? You're focused on your own goals, not the competition. Right?"

"Yeah, pretty much."

"I was trying to figure out how dealing with people wouldn't be personal, even in business situations. How you keep the emotions out of it. But you're not looking at them as competition. Is that how you've been so successful?"

"Perhaps. I think it was more my innate drive to build my own legacy since my father's was denied me."

"That sounds a bit…"

"Over-the-top?" he asked with a grin. "Yeah, I know. But it always felt that way. I'm the third-born son. There was no way I was going to lead the company, and I like my brothers too much to do the kind of things I would have needed to do in order to run it. So I decided to do my own thing and make my company even more successful than Bisset Industries."

There were so many nuances in what he was saying, and it spoke to the complicated family he belonged to. But also to his drive. He was a leader in an industry that was almost out of step with the price-conscious, fast-fashion world they lived in. His American-made brand had been built on old-fashioned values and an aspirational lifestyle that many emulated.

"I get it. I mean, I practice law with my family, but I'm not ever going to be as good as the rest of them, because it's not my passion. That's why I want to make my jewelry business a success, but I haven't found a mentor yet."

"I'm not going to be your mentor beyond this weekend," he said. "It's not my thing. I'll give you some pointers and answer your questions."

"Fair enough," she said. "I figured I'm going to be the one whose coattails you want to ride eventually."

"Damn. I'm never going to live that comment down, am I?" he asked.

"Not for a while," she said. "Actually, I'm glad you said it. It made me seek out more opportunities to put me in competition with you, and it's made me grow my business."

"Then I don't regret it. Competition is where I thrive. So where's this beach you were telling me about?" he asked.

She led him down to the shoreline and away from the crowds. The farther they got from the tourists, the more Leo relaxed. She learned that he liked cherry ice cream, never wore a tank top and read all the Harry Potter books once a year. She told him that she loved butter-pecan ice cream at the beach but chocolate when she was at home. That she loved wearing skirts over shorts and had a huge stack of books that people recommended to her, but she really only read her large collection of romance novels.

They walked along the edge of the water, and she took off her shoes. He glanced around to make sure there wasn't anyone close by—winking at her as he did so—before he took off the deck shoes he wore. The sand was warm under her feet and the water cold. He told her that his youngest brother knew more stories of the sea than anyone else he had met and that, when he was younger, he used to dream of being an only child.

She confessed to the same dream but added that in her version she was a stolen princess whose family searched endlessly for her. Which made him laugh and that made her smile.

She was watching him laugh when something on his face changed and he reached out and snatched the baseball cap off her head. Her hair—always larger in this kind of weather—caught the wind, and she felt the tendrils and curls flying all around. She reached up to capture it, but he caught her hands.

"Leave it," he said. "You look like the ethereal creature I'm slowly realizing you are. Some sort of sea nymph that has soothed something savage inside me."

"I'm not that," she said. And she didn't really believe that there was anything savage about Leo. But it was there in the husky timbre of his voice. "I'm just a girl…well, woman."

"You are so much more," he said, taking her hand and drawing her into his arms.

She put one hand on his chest as his arm went around her waist and he lowered his head. His lips brushed against hers. They were soft yet firm, and when he opened his mouth to deepen the kiss, he tasted better than any man she'd ever kissed. She closed her eyes, felt the wind blowing her curly hair all around their bodies as he kissed her, and she forgot about everything except Leo.

Five

When they started their walk, he definitely hadn't planned on kissing her...but then things had gotten intimate—fast. She'd made him face himself for the first time in a long time. But something about the way she'd gotten past his defenses so quickly made him not trust her. She wasn't what she seemed. But then who was, right?

His mom definitely wasn't who he'd thought she was. He was having a hard time with her betrayal. If it wasn't for her duplicity, he might have been running Bisset Industries, because Logan wouldn't be in the picture. He immediately felt guilty—Logan was in a lot of pain right now and Leo shouldn't be having such jealous, petty thoughts. He guessed he understood why his mother had acted the way she did. And he loved his brother. But still.

His dad—better to not even go there.

And then there was Danni. Sweet Danni with her curly hair that seemed to beckon him to leave behind his cares and his worries. Kind Danni who made those things about himself that had at times felt cringey okay. Sexy Danni who was making this kiss into something more than he'd anticipated. Was she too good to be true? Right now, he didn't care.

There it was. That August Bisset legacy of taking what he wanted without thinking of the consequences to anyone else. Did he really want to be that man? Also how could he stop?

Her hand on his waist held him firmly to her as she went up on her tiptoes and wrapped her other hand around the back of his neck. The kiss deepened and went further than he'd intended.

Her breasts rested against his chest, and he tried to control his response. But he couldn't. He slipped his hand down her back to cup her butt and draw her more fully against him. His erection hardened, and he couldn't help rubbing it against the softness of her tummy.

She tore her mouth from his and looked up at him, though she didn't step back. He wondered what she was thinking, but her eyes were blocked by her dark sunglasses. Her lips were slightly swollen from kissing him, and her hair, that glorious mane of thick, curly hair, was dancing on the wind.

There was something in her that called to him in a way that no other woman had before. She didn't fit his image of where he wanted to go with his life. She was just…a treat, he thought. And he was smart enough to keep that thought to himself.

"I like kissing you," he said.

"I liked it, too," she said.

He felt something under his foot and looked down to see a shell buried in the sand. He stooped down to pick it up, brushing the sand off on his shirt. He handed it to her. "So you won't forget me when you are rich and famous."

She took it from him and pushed her sunglasses up on her head to look at it. "I'll never forget you after you said that crass thing about me in the press."

"I'm trying to make up for it. Give you something else to remember me for," he said. "Hey, I know tonight is the rehearsal dinner, but I am not feeling up to a big party. Would you want to skip it and go on a date with me instead?"

"What did you have in mind? Tonight is my chance to mingle with Toby Osborn and maybe do some networking," she said.

"And you are trying to grow your business," he said. "How about if I take a photo of you on the date that you can use to sell your products?"

"You still haven't said what kind of date it will

be," she said, pushing her sunglasses back down and putting the shell in her pocket.

"My grandmother has a fully restored yacht from the 1930s. It's just the right size for a couple to manage under decent conditions. I'd love to take you sailing and have dinner as the sun sets."

The women Leo had dated over the last ten years had always said he wasn't romantic, but the truth was he'd never made the time to be. In his mind he'd always envisioned a romantic sail with the woman in his life, but he'd never been that far away from a cell phone signal, unable to be reached if a business emergency arose, until today.

As if a cell phone was the only thing making him hesitate. He acknowledged to himself that he wanted her because she was Danni but also she was a distraction. But was he letting himself get too distracted? She hadn't even pretended she didn't want him to mentor her. She had said they were competition and yet…none of that mattered right now.

He'd seen his father focus on building Bisset Industries during his tenure and now the entire family was paying the cost. He needed to believe he was somehow different and that he wouldn't make those mistakes. So one sail…would it be okay?

Today had changed everything, and he had no idea if this was something he'd like or not, but he was tired of not trying. Of filtering everything through what August would do—for maximum personal gain—instead of what Leo wanted to do.

Hell.

He hadn't realized how long he'd been scrambling to get and keep his father's attention. Attention that August was never going to give because Leo was his third son and not a part of Bisset Industries.

"What do you say? I can't promise it will be perfect, but it should be fun," he said at last.

"I'll take fun over perfect every time," she said.

"Good," he said as they started walking back the way they'd come. "I've had a really nice afternoon, Danni. Thank you for that."

"It's my pleasure, Leo. I enjoyed it, too," she said. "I saw an ice cream stand when we were walking here. Do you have time for a snack before you have to get back to your family?"

Leo thought about it. He had responsibilities this weekend. They were all playing a part in the wedding, no matter how big or small. He pulled his phone out of his pocket and saw he'd missed ten messages from his team, who were all back on Long Island. He skimmed them and there weren't any emergencies so he didn't reply. There was one from his mom asking if he was okay, which he also ignored. Instead he texted his cousin to see if she needed him this afternoon at the rehearsal, and her response didn't sound like Adler. It was wooden: just a smiley face and a brief message to enjoy himself. That wasn't Adler. She wrote massively long text messages. Always.

"I'm not sure I can. I want to check on Adler. This new family thing probably has her rattled, too," Leo said. "But I'll see you tonight around six?"

"Okay, see you then," Danni said as they reached town. She turned toward the ice cream stand, waving him up toward the hotel.

He stood there feeling the pull of Danni, but that was ridiculous. He'd only met her this morning. She had no sway over him…but his libido begged to differ.

Danni posted the picture that Leo had helped her stage at the luncheon on her social media accounts and then went to sketch in her art journal. She wanted to capture the day she'd spent with Leo. He stirred emotions in her that she was used to ignoring. She was on the clock if she wanted to make her dreams a reality, and sex wasn't something she normally made time for.

But Leo…the way he'd kissed her made her think of things other than her production schedule and distribution channels. He made her want to be that ethereal woman he'd seen her as on the beach. Someone who lived in the moment, for passion and pleasure.

The truth was she'd never be that woman. But on the pages of her art journal, she could be. She sketched herself the way she always did, but this time as she drew her hair, she didn't feel the resentment she sometimes did toward the long, curly locks. Everyone always envied her, but her hair was hard work, and it was frizzy when she wanted it to be smooth. Though that hadn't mattered to Leo. She sketched him, too, but she wasn't as good with men as she was with women. He looked odd in the picture, so she added a pair of sunglasses over his eyes, and that fixed the problem. She took the shell he'd found for her out of her pocket and flipped to another page in the journal and sketched it from all different angles before she set her journal aside.

She needed to wash her hair before her date with Leo, and it was going to take a while to dry, so if she showered now she might be able to get away without blow-drying it. It was a mundane thing to worry about, but her life was more easily handled when she focused on those details instead of things like her attraction to Leo.

He had been by turns tense and then totally relaxed. And though he'd shared things with her, she knew he was still hiding something. Whatever was going on with his family had shaken Leo to his core. That wasn't the man she'd come to know through his online presence and profile in *Forbes*. He was the kind of man who was always certain, she thought, but this afternoon he hadn't been.

She got out of the shower and then checked her phone to see that it was blowing up with messages from Essie—she had seventy-five text messages waiting. Worried that her friend had been in an accident, she clicked on the thread only to see that Essie was fine. She was texting about their business.

She hit the video chat button to get the down low so she didn't have to scroll through all the messages.

"Where have you been? That photo you posted is blowing up. I mean, we've had more than one hundred orders in the first thirty minutes, and it isn't slowing down," Essie said.

"Sorry, I didn't think we'd get that kind of response. A hundred? Wow, that's great. I bet it will slow down soon. What's our stock like?" she asked. They had a warehouse with products in it, but they were a small business with mainly Danni and three helpers making everything.

"You'd know better than me, but I don't think we can handle more than five hundred orders—not that we will get that many."

"I have two other bracelets that are very similar... let me get to my laptop, and I'll tweak the shop page so that if we sell out, those will pop up as alternatives. And we should set the limit on the back end at four hundred and fifty just to be safe—okay? Once we hit that, we can automatically redirect customers to the other bracelets that I'm thinking of. We have three hundred of each of them. Also we'll set up a button for people to click so they get an email when it's back in stock," Danni said. She felt a fire coursing through her body at the thought of selling stock so quickly. This was exactly why she needed Leo's tutelage: he'd tweaked that photo and helped her sell more bracelets in thirty minutes than she had in the last month.

"Okay, I'll get on it. Dang, girl. This is exciting—stressful, but exciting," Essie said. They continued video chatting while they both worked on updating the website, both front and back end, and then she disconnected with Essie to call her helpers and ask them if they could start working on more bracelets and get them delivered by the following week.

Once she had all that done, she called Essie back and made sure her friend had everything she needed until the next day. She hung up and finished getting ready for her date with Leo, which was coming up soon.

As hot as he was and as much as she wanted him and liked kissing him, she had to focus on continuing to get tips for her business. She wanted to be partnering with luxury brands the way he did. She took out her phone and jotted down things she needed help with in the notepad app. Once she had a solid list, she decided she'd casually bring them up throughout the evening.

She could do that. And she wasn't going to feel guilty about it; he'd told her that he wasn't worried about her business. And it wasn't like she was going to ask him how he got brands to work with him. She knew that developing those relationships would take time, that she needed to get her products noticed so that brands would want her.

He knocked on her door at six, and she opened it and almost forgot her plan. He had on a pair of shorts and a casual collared shirt along with those deck shoes he endorsed. His hair was combed back, and when he smiled at her, she remembered what it had felt like to be in his arms on the beach.

Keeping her mind on business was going to be harder than she had imagined.

Adler Osborn had thought she was getting the wedding of her dreams with a nice, respectable man who came from a well-established family. Nick Williams had the upbringing she'd craved; he'd been raised by two loving parents and was tight with his siblings. Adler had grown up spending half the year on the road with her famous rock star father and the other part of the year with her grandmother and aunt Juliette after her mom had died of a drug overdose. Her father was always in the tabloid headlines and the more that the spotlight had flashed around her, the more Adler had hated it.

So, meeting CEO Nick Williams and falling in love with him was the answer to her long-awaited dream. But then yesterday when her extended family, including her beloved aunt Juliette and her arrogant uncle Auggie, had met Nick's parents, everything had fallen apart. Turns out that Nick was the bastard son of August Bisset. And the fact that the Williams and Bisset families were business rivals and sworn enemies didn't make that matter any easier to handle.

In fact, it was the kind of scandal that had hit TMZ and blown up her picture-perfect, elegant wedding scenario. Then today, when she learned that her cousin Logan was actually not her cousin at all but Nick's twin, things had gone from bad to worse. Nick and Logan hated each other. They were always trying to one-up each other in the boardroom and steal deals out from under each other's noses.

Nick was wigging out and not acting at all like the man she'd fallen in love with, and her Bisset family, her mom's relatives, who could normally be counted on to be calm in a crisis, weren't. They were in the center of a scandal that felt like a hurricane that kept getting bigger and bigger.

When her cousin Leo had offered to come and just chill with her for an hour, she'd jumped at the chance. They'd been close when they were kids, and she liked him. He was funny and sarcastic, and he had a way of cutting through the bullshit and getting straight to the heart of the matter. She had asked everyone to leave her alone for the afternoon to try to process the new family scandal that Logan was actually Nick's twin.

Leo knocked on the door to the hotel suite that she was using to get ready for the wedding, and when she let him in, she noticed his smile didn't go all the way to his eyes.

"Leo? You okay?" she asked. But she knew the situation with his father and Nick's mother had to be affecting Leo, as well. Adler took a deep breath, not sure she was ready to try to play calming influence on another male. Nick was taking all that energy!

"Yes. I'm here for you, kiddo," he said. "I could tell from your very succinct text that you aren't yourself."

She had to laugh at the way he said it. "I knew I should have put more in the message, but I'm out of words. I mean, I have words, but I thought a string of curses followed by *what am I going to do?* would be over-the-top," she said.

He laughed and then pulled her close for a hug. "Maybe for someone else, but not for you, Addie. So, what's going on? Is Nick handling this any better than Logan?"

"No," she said, leading the way farther into the suite and stopping at the bar cart. "Want a drink?"

"I'm good. I have a date later," he said.

"Ooh. With who?" she asked. "I guess that's why you wanted to skip the dinner. I thought it might be because of the other drama. But this is better." Honestly, right now, she had entered a kind of Zen calm about the wedding. She was just too numb to care if people showed up or didn't at the events. Her dream wedding was turning a bit into her worst nightmare and she had other stuff on her mind. If Leo wanted to miss the dinner that was fine with her.

"This is better," he said. "It's with Danni Eldridge."

"I like her, Leo. So, don't do your one-night thing," Adler warned.

"She's a grown woman," Leo said. "I like her, too. She's different."

"She's got a kind heart. We went to school together, and since then her dad became my dad's attorney, and he's one of the toughest lawyers I know. But Danni isn't anything like him," Adler said.

"She mentioned that she's from a family of lawyers. She wants me to give her advice on her business. What made you pick her for your bridal jewelry?" he asked.

"To be honest, I only looked at her stuff because her dad mentioned it to my dad, but then when I saw it…it's really high-quality and so unique. I told her what I wanted, and she sent me back some sketches that were better than I'd imagined," Adler said.

"It is good," Leo said. "You look like you're freaking out again."

She was. The scandal just kept intruding on her thoughts. She wished she could go back to that time before she knew that Nick was August Bisset's biological son. But she couldn't. She was just going to have to keep trying to ignore the tabloid press and paparazzi who were gathering all around the hotel and on Nantucket and pretend that her life was going to be okay.

"I just hate this. I thought I'd picked the kind of man who would give me the nice, quiet life I've always wanted," she said.

"I wish you could have that life, but it's just not in the cards for you. It never has been. You were born in the spotlight, and I can appreciate you trying to have a low-profile wedding, but you're Adler Osborn. That was never going to happen."

"I know," she said. "I'm just glad it's not Dad doing something outrageous."

"Like one of the bridesmaids?" Leo said, arching one eyebrow at her.

They both busted up laughing, because it wasn't that far-fetched that her father would have slept with one or more of the bridesmaids in years past. But he was slowing down with his wild lifestyle and seemed to finally want a life beyond the spotlight.

Leo left a short while later, and Adler felt a bit lighter for having talked to him. She was still concerned about Nick, who wasn't answering her texts and seemed to be questioning all his life choices. She loved him and wanted the wedding to go on, but she wouldn't make a mistake just to keep up appearances. In her mind, marriage was forever.

But she was starting to realize that the man she thought she knew was changing as each new secret from his past was revealed. And in her heart, she was scared that he wouldn't be that forever man she'd always believed him to be.

Six

Leo was an old hand at sailing. As soon as he and Danni were on the yacht and out of the marina, he switched his boat shoes to the old ratty pair he'd mentioned earlier that afternoon. She watched him piloting the yacht and took her sketchbook out to make a rough drawing of him and the boat.

The boat was exquisitely restored and made her feel like she was in one of the glamorous old black-and-white films her mom used to watch on Saturday mornings with her and her siblings. They'd always pile into her parents' king-size bed and drink milky, sweet coffee and watch the old films. The women in them had always been so glitzy and smart, full of sassy comebacks that kept the handsome men on their toes. Danni had loved it.

Leo would have fit very well in one of those old movies. He had the drive and pedigree that the heroes usually had.

He dropped anchor when they were far enough out and not in a line of shipping traffic. It almost seemed as if they were the only two people in the world. The horizon stretched out all around them, and she couldn't help but feeling like he'd somehow had a glimpse inside her secret dreams from the days when she watched those movies and was now making them come true.

He couldn't have, of course, because those dreams were silly in this modern world where everyone was posting constantly. He knew all about that. In the beginning, Leo had built his brand by staging photos showcasing his products and making sure everyone in the world wanted to have his affluent lifestyle. So he was just good at conveying a fantasy, that's all.

"I had Michael pack us dinner," Leo said. "He's my grandmother's butler, and honestly he's usually spot-on when it comes to getting both meals and drinks right. He's famous for his Manhattans, so I asked him to make us a batch…do you like them?"

Not really, but she just shrugged. "I'm not sure I've ever had one. I'm more of a gin and tonic kind of girl. But I'll try it."

"I'm pretty sure the bar in the galley is fully

stocked, so I should be able to whip up whatever you want. Don't feel like you have to drink something just because I suggested it," he said.

"Oh, I don't. I just don't want to start complaining on our first date," she said, realizing that was entirely true. She might have been thinking about peppering the evening with business questions, but that didn't mean she wanted the date to be all business. There was something about Leo that called to a very feminine part of her, and she wanted to explore it.

"First date... I like the sound of that, because it implies there might be more dates," he said, coming over to her and pulling her into his arms. They stood together in the middle of the deck, the ocean breeze blowing around them. His arms wrapped around her made her feel secure and safe. She wasn't a woman who had ever needed someone else to make her feel safe, so that unnerved her a little bit.

"What else did Michael pack for us to eat?" she asked, moving away from him slightly.

Leo didn't mention her move but took the picnic basket he'd brought with them over to the padded benches that lined the bow of the boat. He set it down before opening it and pulling out the items.

"Lobster rolls, homemade coleslaw, sea salt potato chips and some kind of mousse. I told him we wanted something casual."

"Sounds delicious. I swear, every summer I eat more lobster rolls than anything else," she said with a smile, trying to gain back the easy footing they'd had before she'd stepped away from him. She sat down next to the basket so they were facing each other over it.

Leo closed the basket, and it made a tabletop of sorts. "Do you want to try a Manhattan?"

"Yes," she said.

"I'll mix them up. What did you get up to this afternoon?"

Perfect opening for her to mention her business. "I spent most of it on the phone with Essie—she's my business partner. That photo you took of me generated a lot of interest and orders. So, thank you! How did you grow your supply chain? I'm struggling to find quality craftspeople who can work to a deadline."

He mixed up the drinks and then handed one to her. "Supply chain is pretty much hit or miss. I'm a member of the American Crafts Association, and that is a good place to start. There are a lot of artisans in their directory. I will say it's the one area of your business that you don't want to rush. You can look into factory machinery, but I've found that sometimes quality suffers."

"Thanks," she said, taking a sip of her drink. The whiskey was strong but smooth, and the taste wasn't as bad as she recalled. "This is a pretty decent drink."

"I try," he said, then changed the subject. "You

mentioned lobster rolls—what else makes you think of summer?"

"The beach and sunburn. Friday afternoons spent sitting on my porch," she said. "What about you?"

"The beach and being here at Gran's. When we were kids, my mom would pack us all up and we'd spend a month here. Just running around on the beach and in town, sailing, eating…no curfew or rules. It was nice."

"Did you have a lot of rules growing up?" she asked.

"Yes. You?"

"It didn't feel that way, but I know there were limits," she said, realizing how much leeway her parents had always given her. And despite the fact that they'd wanted her to be a lawyer, in all fairness, she'd never really been able to believe she could be anything else until this year. That wasn't her parents' fault.

"Limits are good," he said. "Like maybe only one kiss tonight…otherwise I'm not sure what will happen."

And just like that, he made her realize that she'd backed away earlier because she was afraid that one kiss wouldn't be enough.

Leo had never been known for his tact. He knew bluntly telling Danni he wanted her wasn't the smoothest move, but he wasn't up to being someone he wasn't. He'd seen everything that had happened with his parents today, how all that sophistication they'd always wrapped themselves in had been stripped away. But with Leo, nothing was left but his most basic self. And that man wanted Danni.

He was willing to do what he needed to in order to show her that he wasn't an animal, but really at his core he felt like one. He felt like everything he'd ever believed about himself had been a big rotten husk and now it was gone. He hadn't anticipated shedding it, but nonetheless it was gone.

"Sorry if that was a bit too in-your-face," he said. "But earlier it seemed like you weren't certain you wanted me touching you, and I really don't want to dance around it all night. So, if you're not interested in that, if you just want to be friends or whatever, I'd rather you say it now."

She took a sip of her Manhattan and then crossed her legs before leaning toward him. The sun was behind her as it set, so her face was in shadow. He knew he was pushing, and part of him was doing it because he wanted to see how she was going to react.

"That's straight to the point, isn't it?"

"It is. I'm not really known for being tentative," he reminded her.

"No, you're not. Well, here's the thing. I'm not really into much dating at the moment, because if my business isn't a success by my next birthday, I have to honor my promise to my parents and give it up and go back to practicing law…so there's that. And

I like you. That kiss earlier was hot and I'd like to kiss you again, but…"

He sort of liked the sound of that. He wasn't looking for forever, and a weekend fling sounded perfect right about now.

"But?"

She nibbled her lower lip and shifted back in the seat, resting her arms against the yacht's railings. "You are very complicated. There is nothing straightforward about whatever is going on in your family, and you are the cousin of my client, so that might be odd. But also, I have the feeling that keeping things light with you is going to be hard. And I'm not sure I want to add you to the mix that is my life."

Damn.

He thought he'd dropped a truth bomb, but she had shown him that his wasn't nearly as deep or revealing as hers was. She was being honest. He owed her honesty in return. And he got it. Everything she mentioned was true. He was a mess. His family was crashing and burning in a way that would probably leave scars on them for decades to come. While a weekend fling seemed as if it might be ideal to him, for her it might not be. She would be associated with him, and he didn't want her tainted by this scandal.

"Too much for you?" she asked.

"No. It was exactly what I was fishing for when I said what I did. But I'm trying to decide if we should chuck aside our reservations and go for a weekend fling…or just finish eating dinner and sail back to the marina and walk out of each other's lives."

Danni took a moment, turning away from him to look out over the water. Whatever she came up with, he'd go along with it. He liked her. She was different from the other women he'd dated before and would probably date again after her. But he also cared about her. As Adler had mentioned, Danni had a kind heart, and the last thing he wanted to do was to crush it—even inadvertently.

"Why don't we eat dinner and see where that leads before we make any decisions?"

He nodded. "Sounds good. I wanted the chance to get to know you better."

"Me, too," she said. "Nothing about whatever is going on in your family. Just Leo stuff."

"Leo stuff?" he asked, wiggling his eyebrows at her. "What does that entail?"

"I'm not sure. Things you normally don't talk about for sure, but also what makes you tick."

"Ambition, coffee and the need to prove to my dad that I'm better than him," Leo said. He didn't need to think about that one. He'd been driven by those three things since he'd turned twenty-three and struck out on his own.

Was he still? He wanted to think that nothing had changed in the last few hours, despite the fact that he wanted it to. He wanted to be better than August, but a part of him still wanted his approval.

So stupid.

"That's what makes you tick?" she asked. "What about enjoying the journey? And good friends?"

"I mean, I can give you the politically correct version if you want, but you said to show you the real Leo."

"Fair enough."

"What makes you tick?" he asked.

"I don't know…that's sad, isn't it? I'm almost thirty and really have no idea what it is that is at my core. I know it's not law."

"That's a start," he said.

This, he thought. This was precisely why he needed to be careful of Danni. She was searching for herself, trying to carve her way in the world, and he didn't want to be the man who made her cynical and made her strive for something that Leo was slowly realizing would never be enough even for himself.

"Really?"

"Yes. Just knowing what you don't want to do is a good way to find what you do. You like making bracelets, right? What else?"

What else?

She wasn't sure. That was part of the problem with her life. She wanted not to be a lawyer and wanted to run her own business. But hand-making bracelets was taking her a lot of time to be successful. And when he'd asked if she liked making them…well, she wasn't sure. She'd seen a demo online and tried it. Then someone at the gym saw what she'd made and liked it, so she'd made a bracelet for her, and slowly her business had grown.

But it wasn't like bracelets were her passion.

"I like sketching, but I don't think I can make a living at that," she admitted.

"What kind of living?" he asked. "You have to know what you want so you'll be happy when you get it."

"Do you know?" she asked. "Because you don't seem that happy. Or maybe you haven't gotten there yet."

She knew she sounded defensive. She felt defensive and edgy, but it was only partially to do with him. It was mainly down to herself. She didn't know what she wanted. She loved her condo in the city, but it wasn't her dream home. She enjoyed the challenge of growing her business and forging her own path, but was it her higher purpose? Her mind was jumbled with images of different things she'd like to achieve in life.

He lifted both hands to her shoulders. "I do know what makes me happy, but once I get there—once I achieve it—then I want something else. So maybe… maybe I don't know what makes me happy."

She nodded. "Me neither. Sorry if I came across as aggressive. I hate that I'm not surer of my life."

"Honestly, I don't think many people are. By any

definition, I'd be considered successful, yet there is still something missing in my life," he said. "Some hole that hasn't been filled."

"I can't believe that," she said. "You have everything. I can't think of a single pleasure, home, car, boat, that you don't have."

"I don't have my own plane," he admitted.

"Is that important?"

"No, or I would have bought one," he said, winking at her. "Just kidding. You're right, though. I have enough stuff, but still I'm looking for something else."

"Love?" she asked.

He started laughing. "Uh, no. That's a fairy tale."

"Is it? What about Adler and Nick?"

"I don't know. Most of the people I know who love each other usually end up hurting each other. I'm not interested in that."

Wow. She'd never thought of love that way. Her mom and dad were still in love with each other. They fought at times, but they were definitely the kind of couple she wanted to be when she settled down. And her sister had been in love with the same woman for ten years, and they'd been married for five.

"I guess I see love differently. You're not supposed to hurt someone if you love them."

"It's not always hurting someone else. Love hurts the person who is experiencing it. It might not be something malicious, you know. Love is…it's like a storm at sea. Unpredictable, and it tends to leave nothing but flotsam behind."

"Leo, that's not love," she said. "I'm not going to pretend to be an expert. But love is supporting someone when you know they're making a mistake, and love is smiling because you see each other—"

"For you, maybe." He cleaned up the remains of their dinner and stood up. "We'll have to agree to disagree."

"Sure," she said. But a part of her realized that she wanted to show him good love. But she wasn't getting involved with him. She might hook up with him because she wanted to, but that would be it.

"What's next on the agenda?" she asked.

"You want to stay out here for a bit?" he asked. "Once the sun sets, we can swim under the stars. Night swimming is my favorite."

"I'd like that. Luckily, I have my swimsuit in my bag," she said.

"Thinking ahead. I like it. Sorry I got a little—"

"Don't be. We're just getting to know each other. There are going to be buttons we aren't even conscious we are pushing."

He put his hands on his hips and looked over at her. "I can't decide if you're a genius or not."

"Of course I'm a genius," she said with a laugh. "I'll go and change into my bathing suit."

"Yell before you come up. I'll change up here."

She nodded and went down the gangway, carrying her bag with her. She wasn't as smart as she'd been bragging. If she were, she'd have been asking him business management questions instead of debating love.

Love. She wasn't an expert. She'd never loved anyone except maybe her family. But that was different. It bothered her that he thought love was hurtful, though.

It told her a lot about his personal relationships, and she factored that into what he'd said about business not being personal...no wonder it wasn't to him. It was more than likely his business relationships were more stable than his personal ones.

Did she want to get caught up in that? She was on the clock to get her business off the ground. Leo had so much to offer her with his knowledge, connections and business instinct. Another woman might be able to ignore her feelings and get what she needed but Danni had never been that way.

She changed into her swimsuit. It was a one-piece; she'd just never felt comfortable in a bikini. She didn't look at herself in the mirror—the temptation to see flaws was great, even though she knew the suit flattered her. Her brother had told her once that men didn't judge women the way women did, and she was her own worst critic.

She shrugged and yelled up, getting the all-clear before she went back up to find Leo standing at the edge of the deck looking out at the ocean. He'd taken off his shirt and wore only his swim trunks. She caught her breath at the sight of him. He was too much to handle in her life right now, if she was being honest, but at the same time, she knew she wasn't going to just turn and walk away.

Every new thing she learned about him made him more intriguing. She might not know what she wanted to achieve, but she knew she wanted Leo.

Seven

The water was colder than she expected. She took a quick dip and got out to lie on the deck on her towel. Leo did the same. The evening air was summery and warm. She tried to keep her eyes off his body, but he had really well-developed pecs, which were always her weak spot. His stomach was flat but not wash-board lean. He looked good, like a normal man instead of some kind of perfect Hollywood specimen.

She had reviewed her notes when getting changed, and there were a lot of business questions she should be asking him. Except she kept getting distracted. He was lying on his side next to her. So close. His eyes seemed bluer than they had before. The sun was slowly setting, and there was something in his body language that made business the very last thing she wanted to concentrate on.

"So far if I had to rate this date, I'd give myself a failing grade," he said. "A cocktail you don't like, a freezing-cold swim and a rant about love…you're not getting the best version of Leo tonight."

She smiled and shook her head. "I like this version of Leo. He's not perfect. I mean, your social media feed and press image made it seem like you're someone who always has his stuff together."

Leo groaned. "I'm not sure I like where this is heading. I scrolled through your social feed earlier, and I know you didn't ask for my advice, but your feed is all over the place. You have some really good images and content, but you need a focus."

"You think so? I'm never sure if I should curate my content more carefully or be authentic," she admitted. "I don't want to come across as constantly trying to hawk my products."

"Listen, if people are following you, it's because they like your products. So, you need to give them content that builds on that. Just giving you a tip. Ultimately, you should do what you want and what makes you feel comfortable," he said.

As the sun set, the breeze felt colder against her skin, giving her goose bumps. She shivered, and Leo rubbed her arm. "Is it too cold?"

"It is chilly, but I'm not uncomfortable yet."

"Yet…"

"I mean, once the sun goes down, I might need to grab my sweatshirt," she said.

"Do you have one with you?"

"Yes. I know it's silly to carry such a big bag, but when I'm at the beach I find I need a few wardrobe essentials. I don't like to be caught unprepared."

"Me neither," he said. "I put our dessert below if you want to go down there. We can eat and chat."

Eat and chat. It sounded so innocuous and not at all what she thought Leo Bisset usually did on dates with women. But she wasn't his usual gal. She knew that. As he'd said, as far as first dates went, this one wasn't going to go down in the history books as the best one. She thought he might have decided that they were going to be quasi friends for the weekend. With no shot at being lovers.

She ignored the twinge of disappointment that went through her. That was for the best. She needed to keep her cool and focus on her real life, which was more about getting her company to make a big enough profit so she could keep doing what she wanted to do.

"What's the matter?" he asked.

"Nothing. Why?"

"Your face…you don't look as excited to be here as you were earlier."

She thought about it for a moment, weighing whether or not she should tell him what she was thinking, but she'd never really been good at hiding her thoughts. And what did she have to lose?

"I'm not sure if you've changed your mind about this date," she admitted. "I guess I was starting to enjoy Leo the man and getting to know the real you. I mean, tonight I think I'm seeing the ratty-canvas-shoe side of you instead of the polished, preppy, jet-setting man that the world knows. I liked it. I don't want you to shove me away with the rest of the crowd."

She realized after she said it that she hadn't left herself anywhere to retreat to. She was all in suddenly, and that was exciting and scary. She had no idea what his reaction was going to be, and a part of her was okay with that even though she normally liked to tread carefully.

"I don't want to push you away, either. I just figured after my many screwups that we should write this night off and maybe start over another time," he said.

"I think the screwups are what makes this feel more real."

"Me, too," he said as he reached out and ran his hand along the side of her face, then down her neck. Shivers spread down her body from his touch. It was as intense as that moment earlier on the beach when he'd kissed her.

Leo's touch seemed to be calibrated to her body. Every brush of his fingers or his gaze on her made her react as if she'd been awakened from a long sleep. She leaned slightly toward him, her lips parting. She didn't want dessert or more conversation, she wanted Leo. She wanted his arms around her and his bare chest pressed against hers. She wanted his big, strongly muscled arms wrapped around her and his mouth on hers.

She scooted slightly closer to him, and he leaned in, as well. She felt the brush of his breath over her cheek and then his lips against hers. She parted them and let him in, realizing she'd missed the taste of him over the few hours since she'd last kissed him.

He put one arm under her shoulders and the other over her waist and drew her into the curve of his body as he deepened the kiss.

Danni tasted like the sea and summer, and this kiss made him realize that he had grown complacent in his life. Maybe this entire thing with his parents was the wake-up call he needed. Because he knew without that situation, he wouldn't have taken Danni out tonight.

He just didn't take time out for himself. The question was always: How does this move my brand forward and how can I use this to take over a better position in the global marketplace?

He would have missed this. Missed the taste of her as her hungry mouth moved under his. The feel of her as her curvy body nestled in closer, her breasts pushing against his chest, her belly brushing against his stomach.

He wanted so much more from her, and he wasn't a man used to denying himself, so he didn't do so now. She wrapped one of her arms around his shoulders, drawing herself closer to him. He rolled over and realized he could have picked a better place to start this than on the deck of the yacht. He shifted her in his arms and then sat up. She adjusted her legs until she sat crossways on his lap. Her fingers pushed into his hair, and she held the back of his head as their eyes met.

He tried to remember what it was he'd been trying to do when all he really wanted to do was kiss her again. And not stop until he was buried deep inside her body. She was making him forget the chaos that had become his life.

He lowered his head, but before he could kiss her, he felt the brush of her tongue against his lips, moving over them and tracing the outline. He got hard all at once, and he groaned as she straddled him, her leg brushing against his erection.

She had both her hands on his head, holding him still as she took her time exploring his mouth. Her kiss was thorough and made him harder. It didn't allow him any time to do anything other than try to figure out the quickest way to get her naked…which made him pause.

He leaned back to break the kiss, and she arched one eyebrow at him.

"Is there a problem?"

"Yeah. I don't have a condom with me," he said. To be honest, as much as he wanted Danni, Leo hadn't been sure that sex was the right move between them. But now that didn't seem to matter. He wished he'd just brought one with him.

"It's not a problem. I'm on the pill," she said. "And I'm healthy. Are you?"

He nodded. "Had to have a physical last month for my company. Good. I'm glad."

"I'm glad, too," she said. "I would have thought you'd bring a condom."

"I didn't want to presume, and if I had one…well, let's just say I'd rather it be your choice than my pressuring you into it," he said.

She shifted slightly so she could whisper in his ear. "Do you feel pressured?"

He groaned. Whatever he'd expected of Danni when it came to sex, it was this sensual playfulness that was turning him on and making him realize that he might not have a lot of control where she was concerned.

"I feel horny."

She laughed. The sound was pure joy, and he couldn't help pulling her back and kissing her to try to capture some of her joie de vivre himself. But it quickly melted into desire. Her bathing suit and his swim trunks were thin barriers, and he knew she had to be able to feel his erection between her legs. She swiveled her hips against it, riding him through his trunks, and he couldn't help the guttural noise he made.

He put his hands on her butt to stop her from grinding against him but then found himself pushing her down on his shaft. He slipped his fingers beneath the cloth of her bathing suit, caressing her butt as she moved.

She was kissing him again, and he honestly felt like he could die in her arms and he'd be okay with it. He never wanted this feeling of anticipation to end. She rocked against him, his fingers moving over her butt, tracing her crack until he couldn't take it any longer. He wanted her naked.

He wanted to see her breasts, taste her nipples. He eased the strap of her one-piece bathing suit down her shoulder, and she moved back to stand over him, her legs on either side of his thighs.

He let his gaze move up her legs, to her body and her one breast that was now exposed. She took the other strap off, pushed her suit down over her waist and legs, and stepped out of it. She stood over him, a naked Venus risen from the sea of his dreams to distract and tempt him.

He shifted to his knees, put his hands on her thighs, kissing them as he moved higher. Using the fingers of one hand, he parted her and rubbed his tongue over her clit. Her hands were on his head, pushing him closer to her, and he made a meal of her delicate flesh. Tasting her and driving her arousal higher and higher with each flick of his tongue. Her hands tightened in his hair, and he put one of his hands on her butt cheek, drawing her even closer as he continued to taste her.

She gasped his name; it was a high, breathy sound. He could tell she was getting close to her orgasm, felt the bud beneath his tongue swelling with each brush, and he shoved his finger up inside her as he gently bit down on her clit.

She screamed his name. Her legs went weak, and he caught her as she collapsed in his arms.

Danni's entire body was buzzing as Leo lifted her in his arms and carried her to the padded bench where they'd eaten dinner. He shoved his swim trunks down his legs. She caught her breath at the sight of his fully erect manhood. She reached out and touched him, took him in her hand and caressed him.

She'd had a hunch making love to him was going to be more intense than anything she'd experienced before. He'd been raw and real with her when they talked and ate, and just now he had pushed that even further.

She'd never had filters with lovers—didn't see the point in pretending to be someone she wasn't. She hadn't ever faked an orgasm with a guy, because she felt like that just made him think he was a better lover than he really was. But with Leo there had been no time to think. No need to do the little tricks she normally had to do in order to get herself to come. He'd pushed straight past all her barriers and wrapped her in a web of sensuality, need and longing that had driven out everything except the feelings he was stirring in her.

He sat down and brought her down on his lap. His hands went to her breasts as she straddled him and felt his erection nudging at her center. She shifted so that she could feel him at her core, but he stopped her. "Not yet. I want the chance to explore every part of you in case I screw up later."

She put her hands on either side of his face and looked into his eyes. There was an honesty there that ripped right through her. "I want that, too. You won't screw up."

"Don't. I'm not sure what I'm doing right now. I just know that I can't let you go," he said, then seemed to regret his words. He pulled her head down to his, his tongue pushing deep into her mouth. It tasted faintly salty from her. That thought made another pulse of desire go through her, and she reached down to take him into her hand and rub the tip of his cock against her center. She pushed her hips forward and down until she was impaled on him. She stayed still. This was what she'd needed. She'd felt so empty without him inside her.

"Now you can take your time," she whispered in his ear. "I needed you inside me."

He groaned and uttered a curse word as he put his hands on her backside and drove up into her. "Now I can't. I have to finish this."

He tried to bring her along with him. He teased her, bent to capture her nipple in his mouth, and she threw her head back as she rode him hard. He thrust again and again until he tore his mouth from her breast and buried his head in the side of her neck, sucking at her skin as she felt him come inside her just a moment before she came again. Her orgasm made lights dance behind her eyes, and she shivered and continued riding him until her climax passed.

She slumped forward in his arms, resting her head on his shoulder as he ran his hand up and down her back. He held her loosely to him as his breathing slowed. He didn't make any move to shift her off his lap, and she was content to stay where she was. Over his shoulder she saw the last rays of the setting sun.

He'd given her a summer memory that she knew would last forever. He started to move, and she pushed herself delicately off his lap and then stood there for a second. When their eyes met, the rawness she'd glimpsed before was gone, and the smooth billionaire was back in its place.

"You can clean up in the head downstairs first. I'll give you some privacy."

She stood there for a moment, unwilling to believe

he was dismissing her, but it felt that way. Like he was tired of her and needed some distance.

"Is something wrong?" she asked. Then immediately wished she hadn't. Why couldn't she have just gone below deck and gotten changed instead of poking at him? But she knew the answer. She wasn't a woman who took lovers lightly. She knew this would more than likely be a fling, but she wasn't going to allow him to treat her as if she didn't matter. As if she could just be sent off when he was done with her.

"Everything is wrong, Danni. We're strangers, yet that sex was deeper and more…hell, I don't know what. But it was more. I'm not sure what's going on, and every time I open my mouth on this date, I make a mess of things. I figured you needed some time to yourself."

She reached over and pulled him into her arms, hugging him tightly to her. "It's the same for me. It scares mc, the emotions you're stirring inside me," she admitted. "I know that no matter what we both say, this thing between us is only for one weekend, but at the same time, it feels like it could be more."

He turned his head and looked into her eyes.

"It can't be. I'm not a forever kind of man."

"And you don't believe in love," she said. "I do. And that's a nonnegotiable for me."

Eight

Being back in his grandmother's house and away from Danni made him realize how on edge he truly was. Dare was sitting on the patio in the backyard, holding an unlit cigarette in his hand, as was his oldest brother's habit. Dare was a senator and had spent his entire life being groomed for public service. There was a part of Leo that had never understood Dare's need to do that, but it was something his brother was called to do.

His father loved having what he considered an insider on Capitol Hill. But Dare seldom voted for big business's interests and often put the little guy first, something that had led to many fights between August and Dare.

"Did I miss much tonight?" he asked.

"Yeah," Dare said. "Let's see. Zac sang to Iris and won her back with some heartfelt lyrics and help from Toby."

"Glad to hear it," Leo said. Zac had entered into an arrangement with the maid of honor to be her date for the weekend in exchange for financial backing. Over the time he got to know Iris, he'd fallen in love with her. But he'd let it slip out that she'd paid him to be her date, and it had been picked up by the gossip sites, which had caused a huge problem for Iris, who was a brand influencer who had her own show about relationships and weddings. So it had been damaging. Since then, Zac had been trying to make amends and win her back.

"Adler lost her cool and I'm not sure if Nick can fix the problems between them. Dad didn't show up. He's locked in the study with Carlton. And Mom went to talk Adler off the ledge and was instrumental in keeping her on Nantucket."

Leo dropped down next to his brother on one of the loungers that offered a view of the ocean and Gran's garden. "I guess we shouldn't be surprised that every event is highly charged. If I were Adler and Nick, I think I'd elope."

"Right? But at this point I think there are too many people here for them to even entertain that idea. Where were you, by the way?" Dare asked.

Leo rubbed the back of his neck. He wasn't sure

Treat Yourself with 2 Free Books!

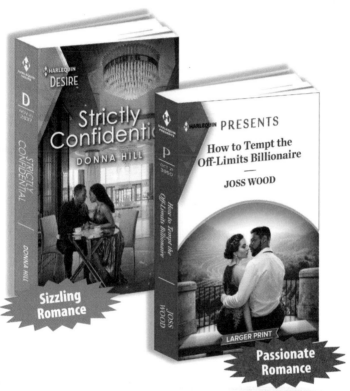

Sizzling Romance

Passionate Romance

GET UP TO 4 FREE BOOKS & 2 FREE GIFTS WORTH OVER $20

See Inside For Details

Claim Them While You Can

Get ready to relax and indulge with your FREE BOOKS and more!

Claim up to FOUR NEW BOOKS & TWO MYSTERY GIFTS – absolutely FREE!

Dear Reader,

We both know life can be difficult at times. That's why it's important to treat yourself so you can relax and recharge once in a while.

And I'd like to help you do this by sending you this amazing offer of up to FOUR brand new full length FREE BOOKS that WE pay for.

This is everything I have ready to send to you right now:

Try **Harlequin® Desire** books featuring the worlds of the American elite with juicy plot twists, delicious sensuality and intriguing scandal.

Try **Harlequin Presents® Larger-Print** books featuring the glamorous lives of royals and billionaires in a world of exotic locations, where passion knows no bounds.

Or **TRY BOTH!**

All we ask in return is that you answer 4 simple questions on the attached Treat Yourself survey. You'll get **Two Free Books** and **Two Mystery Gifts** from each series you try, *altogether worth over $20!* Who could pass up a deal like that?

Sincerely,

Pam Powers

Harlequin Reader Service

Treat Yourself to Free Books and Free Gifts.

Answer 4 fun questions and get rewarded.

	YES	NO
1. I LOVE reading a good book.	○	○
2. I indulge and "treat" myself often.	○	○
3. I love getting FREE things.	○	○
4. Reading is one of my favorite activities.	○	○

TREAT YOURSELF • Pick your 2 Free Books...

Yes! Please send me my Free Books from each series I select and Free Mystery Gifts. I understand that I am under no obligation to buy anything, as explained on the back of this card.

Which do you prefer?
- ❏ **Harlequin Desire®** 225/326 HDL GRAN
- ❏ **Harlequin Presents®** Larger-Print 176/376 HDL GRAN
- ❏ **Try Both** 225/326 & 176/376 HDL GRAY

FIRST NAME	LAST NAME

ADDRESS

APT.#	CITY

STATE/PROV.	ZIP/POSTAL CODE

EMAIL ❏ Please check this box if you would like to receive newsletters and promotional emails from Harlequin Enterprises ULC and its affiliates. You can unsubscribe anytime.

HD/HP-520-TY22

▶ DETACH AND MAIL CARD TODAY!

HARLEQUIN Reader Service —**Here's how it works:**

Accepting your 2 free books and 2 free gifts (gifts valued at approximately $10.00 retail) places you under no obligation to buy anything. You may keep the books and gifts and return the shipping statement marked "cancel." If you do not cancel, approximately one month later we'll send you more books from the series you have chosen, and bill you at our low, subscribers-only discount price. Harlequin Presents® Larger-Print books consist of 6 books each month and cost $5.80 each in the U.S. or $5.99 each in Canada, a savings of at least 11% off the cover price. Harlequin Desire® books consist of 6 books each month and cost just $4.55 each in the U.S. or $5.24 each in Canada, a savings of at least 13% off the cover price. It's quite a bargain! Shipping and handling is just 50¢ per book in the U.S. and $1.25 per book in Canada.* You may return any shipment at our expense and cancel at any time — or you may continue to receive monthly shipments at our low, subscriber-only discount price plus shipping and handling. *Terms and prices subject to change without notice. Prices do not include sales taxes which will be charged (if applicable) based on your state or country of residence. Canadian residents will be charged applicable taxes. Offer not valid in Quebec. Books received may not be as shown. All orders subject to approval. Credit or debit balance in a customer's account(s) may be offset by any other outstanding balance owed by or to the customer. Please allow 3 to 4 weeks for delivery. Offer available while quantities last. **Your Privacy** – Your information is being collected by Harlequin Enterprises ULC, operating as Harlequin Reader Service. For a complete summary of the information we collect, how we use this information and to whom it is disclosed, please visit our privacy notice located at https://corporate.harlequin.com/privacy-notice. From time to time we may also exchange your personal information with reputable third parties. If you wish to opt out of this sharing of your personal information, please visit www.readerservice.com/consumerschoice or call 1-800-873-8635. **Notice to California Residents** – Under California law, you have specific rights to control and access your data. For more information on these rights and how to exercise them, visit https://corporate.harlequin.com/california-privacy.

BUSINESS REPLY MAIL
FIRST-CLASS MAIL   PERMIT NO. 717   BUFFALO, NY

POSTAGE WILL BE PAID BY ADDRESSEE

HARLEQUIN READER SERVICE
PO BOX 1341
BUFFALO NY 14240-8571

If offer card is missing write to: Harlequin Reader Service, P.O. Box 1341, Buffalo, NY 14240-8531 or visit www.ReaderService.com ▶

NO POSTAGE
NECESSARY
IF MAILED
IN THE
UNITED STATES

he wanted to talk about Danni, but this was Dare. Of all the Bissets, Dare was the most levelheaded and had a way of looking at a problem that always brought clarity.

"I went on a date," he said. "After having words with Dad, the last thing I really wanted was more family drama. I visited with Adler to make sure she'd be okay with it."

"I'm not going to scold you for missing the rehearsal dinner," Dare said.

"I did sound defensive, didn't I?" He had to admit when the family was all together, it was sometimes a little too easy to fall back into the sibling dynamic they'd had growing up. Leo, Zac, and Mari often seemed like the troublemakers while Logan and Dare had to step in and be sensible. But Logan wasn't himself right now, and that left only Dare to hold them all together.

"A tad, but I don't blame you. By the way, I am not a fan of how you talked to Dad this afternoon, but I think you were spot-on with your message. He's spent too many years selfishly pushing us all, including Mom, into the roles he wants for us and never once has acknowledged the price we've paid."

Leo looked over at Dare. "I realize I was harsh, but honestly, it was a sobering moment for me. You know I've always craved Dad's respect and kudos, and today...well, I had the first inkling that maybe

I was Don Quixote, tilting at windmills instead of pursuing something real."

"I get it. I think Mari had the same realization not that long ago, and my relationship with Dad was always complex, so I keep my distance when I can. But I think he's finally starting to understand the impact of his focus on always being the best…it's not even the best. What would you say it was?"

"He thinks he's better than everyone else. That he can do whatever he wants and there won't be any consequences," Leo said. "And this weekend he's learned otherwise."

"We all have. It's made me think hard about my actions," Dare said.

"Really? What have you ever done that is questionable?" Leo asked.

Dare looked uncomfortable as he glanced away. "Never mind that. How was your date?"

How was it? Leo still wasn't sure. He'd dropped Danni off at her place, and she'd been sweet when they'd said their goodbyes. A part of him had wanted to stay the night, but after their discussion on the yacht, he knew that wasn't wise. They'd both acknowledged they weren't in a position to start a relationship, and if he'd stayed…it wouldn't have been the wise thing to do.

"That bad? Or that good?" Dare asked. "It's taking you a long time to answer."

Leo laughed and shook his head. "Both. Can it

be both? She's complicated, Dare. She brings out my most real self, and that guy isn't as polished as I'm used to being. I feel like I have no game when I'm with her. And then something unexpected will happen and we connect…"

"That's good, Lion," Dare said, using Leo's childhood nickname. "It means that you are probably with a woman who is going to change your life. Tell me more about her. What does she do?"

"She's got a small Etsy shop to sell her jewelry and leather goods. I pretty much dissed her in an interview and then of course she was in the foursome at the scramble. But…there's something about her."

"You don't sound like you. I think that's good," Dare said.

"Is she? Or is it just that everything with Mom and Dad has me in a tailspin?" Leo asked. "I'm so confused about everything. No one is who I thought they were, and for the first time ever, I don't respect Dad. I mean, he's always been tough and, as you said, arrogant. But I kind of got why up until today. Today when I heard Mom talking about how he was when she was pregnant…he just seemed like a bully, and I don't want to be that kind of man."

Dare tucked the unlit cigarette into his shirt pocket and spun around to face him. Leo stared up at his older brother and waited.

"You're never going to be that kind of man," Dare said. "Dad would never be able to honestly look at himself the way you are. And I think the woman you went out with is more important to you than you want to admit."

"Maybe."

Dare didn't say anything else, just squeezed Leo's shoulder before going into the house. Leo stayed where he was, thinking about Danni and if there was a way forward with her or if he should just let himself be satisfied with one night.

Danni took a shower and then climbed into her bed, taking her sketchbook with her. There were so many images tumbling around in her head after the date with Leo. She'd toyed with asking him in when he'd walked her back to her cottage, but in the end, she had decided that she didn't need to do anything else spontaneous. She needed to remember her focus, her goal. She didn't know how Essie did it, but her friend never seemed to really have any problem staying in complete boss babe mode.

Danni vacillated between wanting to be a titan of industry and needing to curl up with her sketchbook. Or, in the case of this evening, curling up with Leo. She hadn't asked him in, but she missed him. She found her pencil moving over the page and saw the images she was sketching were all him. He'd been so…all man. Normally he had a sophisticated polish that made everyone in the room notice him. Men wanted to be him, and women wanted to be with him.

But tonight, when he'd stood on the deck of the yacht, she'd had a glimpse of a different man. Probably the reason why he was so successful in business was because he had that wildness inside him.

She realized that he had a killer instinct. Something that she'd been told to develop by many of the TED talks she'd watched and business seminars she'd attended. Actually, her father had advised it as well for when she was in the courtroom, but that wasn't her. It just never had been.

She closed the sketchbook, realizing that staring at drawings of Leo wasn't what she needed to do. She opened the notes app on her phone and looked at the list she'd made before her date with Leo. He had given her a few tips and she was glad of that; she would use them when moving forward, but she still needed to learn so much more from him.

She had one more chance tomorrow at the wedding, but honestly, how was she going to turn the topic to business advice at the reception? She doubted she'd get a chance to talk to him at the ceremony. And honestly, should she even continue on this path?

When she thought back over the night, she realized he'd just volunteered info that would help her with the business. But she wasn't very good at shutting down her emotions and just getting the information she needed. Maybe she needed to be more like that. But how?

She rubbed the back of her neck, enjoying how

parts of her body were pleasantly sore from Leo's lovemaking. She felt a tingle between her legs as she remembered his mouth on her. She definitely regretted not inviting him in now.

He seemed like the kind of man who would have wanted sex again, and she realized she wanted him now.

She rolled over. Was she finally turning into a sexual creature? After all these years of just sort of liking sex, she was now obsessively reliving every moment on the yacht with Leo. He'd brought out a side of her that she hadn't really given much weight in the past, and she wanted to be more of that woman.

She got out of bed and went into the living room. Getting out her laptop, she forced herself to work. She was on Nantucket to grow her business and to keep her client happy. Not to develop an obsession with Leo Bisset.

She opened up the order page on the website and saw that they had reached capacity on the bracelets. She was both thrilled and surprised but also a little worried. She had to sort out her supply-chain issues if she was going to take her business to the next level.

She was trying to concentrate on that when her phone pinged, and she glanced over at the notification on the screen, expecting the message to be from Essie. But it was Leo. She picked up her phone and read it.

I know you're probably sleeping but I can't. I miss you.

She thought about ignoring it, but she couldn't.

Not sleeping. Trying to work to take my mind off you. This is so crazy. We're practically strangers.

She saw the dancing dots and waited for his response, closing her laptop and curling her legs underneath her. She didn't have long to wait.

It is crazy, but I like it. My family are all sleeping, and I don't know if I can.

Why not? she immediately responded.

Thinking of you and...

And?

I said some douchey things to my dad and mom earlier and I'm not sure what to expect when I see them in the morning.

Best to just apologize...do you think you should?

Yes. But I'm still mad so I'm afraid I might say something else hurtful. And tomorrow is the wedding so I should try to just be chill.

Is there anything I can do?

Run away with me. Jk. I can't do that. And I know you wouldn't.

Danni sent back the zany face emoji, but a part of her wished he'd meant it. But she was starting to suspect that it wasn't her—Danni Eldridge—that Leo was obsessed with at this moment. It almost seemed as if any woman would do. She was just holding a place, being the distraction he needed. It was the distraction that he wanted and not really her. She realized she had to be very careful not to make Leo into a man she wanted him to be but that he wasn't.

I have to go now, she typed. See you at the ceremony tomorrow.

Okay. Good night.

Good night.

She put her phone away, knowing she'd done the right thing. No matter how intense and real the feelings between herself and Leo were, she was wise enough to know that a man who didn't believe in love wasn't going to fall for her.

Juliette Bisset was sleeping in the same room as her husband, in the same queen-size bed they always shared when visiting her mother. But it felt bigger than king-size. She was careful to stay to her own side and had been pretending to sleep since Auggie had come into the room.

She hadn't been able to talk to Logan; he was refusing all conversations with her, and her heart was breaking.

The secret of his birth had always been tucked deep inside her. From the moment she'd held him and then breastfed him, Logan had been her son. As he'd grown up, he hadn't seemed any different from her other children, and she'd believed that the secret of his birth would be one she'd take to her grave. But she should have known better.

She felt tears burning her eyes and struggled to keep her breathing even so Auggie wouldn't hear her crying. But when he rolled over and put his hand on her shoulder, she let out the ragged breath that she'd been holding. She didn't know what to say to him or to her kids. She was sorry she'd kept Logan's birth a secret, but she'd been convinced the only way to keep her marriage together was to bring home a healthy son to Auggie, and a part of her had been proven right. They had gotten stronger as a couple after that. It was only after Leo's birth, when Auggie had a public affair, that she'd realized she might have been lying to herself for years. But at that point, with four sons, she'd felt like she had no choice but to stay with him.

"Jules…"

"Don't," she said. Her voice was ragged, and no matter how much she wanted to stop crying, she couldn't. "I can't talk about this."

He pulled her into his arms, curving against her back and just holding her, which made her cry that much harder. She'd always struggled with why she stayed with him for all these years, but this was the very reason why. There were times when August was the best man she'd ever known. Of course, he was also the worst man she'd ever known. It was a constant balancing act. After Mari's birth they'd found a new truce, and over the last twenty years, they'd really fallen in love and committed themselves to each other and their marriage. Or so Juliette had thought.

"I'm sorry," he said. "I know you don't want to talk about this, but I'm very sorry that you went through the loss of our son alone and that you felt as if you had no other choice than to bring another baby home in his place."

She shook her head. "Me, too."

"Where did you bury our son?" he asked her.

She had been keeping this secret for too long. She'd had the baby cremated and put his ashes in an urn that she'd kept hidden here at her mom's house until Musette had died. Her broken, lost sister, who wouldn't be there to see her daughter grow up, and Juliette's lost son were buried together in the family plot on the property.

"Here, in the family plot with Musette. I figured my lost sister and son should be together."

"That sounds about right," he said. "Honey—"

"Don't *honey* me. Not right now, Auggie. I can't…"

"Okay."

She didn't say anything else and neither did he, leaving her wondering if he'd fallen asleep. But then he squeezed her tight. "I'm sorry I was such an ass for so many years. You were always too good for me."

"Now I'm sure you don't feel that way," she said. She'd deceived him for a long time, and that had to rankle him and make him mad at her. Though the way he held her made her believe that he wasn't upset with her after all.

"I do still feel that way. It makes me realize my influence on you… I always hoped you'd make me a better man and never thought how I would affect you. My behavior changed you. Made you afraid for our family. I don't want you to think that I didn't love you and Dare and our unborn child. The affair…well, sometimes I think it was my way of proving I was still a stud. Still the biggest, baddest man in the room, never realizing that I was sacrificing what mattered."

She didn't want to hear any of that. August was looking back on that time with regret, as he should do, but Juliette remembered how it was, and the pain was still very sharp. He'd needed to be the man every woman wanted, and he'd had a string of affairs around the time of each of her pregnancies. It seemed that as much as he wanted to build a dynasty, at the same time each new child was a bond that tied him closer to her, and he'd resented that. He'd wanted to be seen as his own man.

He rolled her over to face him. His face wasn't clear in the dappled moonlight coming into the room, but decades of sleeping with the man made it easy for her to discern his strong features. Age had added lines by his eyes and mouth, and gray at his temples, but she still saw the man she'd fallen in love with all those years ago.

"Why did you stay with me?" he asked.

"Did you want me to leave you? Was that why you had the affairs?" she asked. She'd often wondered if her own stubbornness in not just leaving and letting her marriage fail had made her equally culpable in their relationship.

"No, I didn't. But I did have a lot of guilt. Thinking you were better than me," he admitted.

"But now you know I wasn't," she said. "I didn't leave you because when you turn that charm and attention on me, you make me feel like I'm the only woman in the world that matters to you. I guess we both know that was never true."

"Jules," he said.

But she was already turning her back to him, and

after a moment, she heard him get up and leave the room. She didn't cry anymore, but sleep eluded her for the rest of the night.

Nine

Saturday dawned bright and sunny, almost as if to make up for the hovering storm cloud of paparazzi and scandal-sheet reporters in the lobby of the Nantucket Hotel.

Danni made her way through the lobby to the elevators, carrying a box of doughnuts and a thermos of coffee. She was headed up to meet Adler and her bridal party. To be honest, Danni wasn't sure she was needed, but she had wanted to ensure that Adler was beyond happy with not only her product but with her customer service. So, when Adler had texted to ask if she minded stopping by the bakery and bringing doughnuts and coffee to the suite, Danni had texted back an enthusiastic "of course." She didn't mind and would love to do it.

She was here for business. In fact, last night she should have been schmoozing at the rehearsal dinner instead of going on a date with Leo. She'd heard that Toby Osborn had given an unscheduled performance. The two people who were talking about it in front of her in line at the doughnut shop mentioned that some of his music industry friends had been there, too.

A part of Danni had wondered if maybe she should be going after that crowd for business. She hated to think in clichés, but most musicians did wear a lot of jewelry. But she wasn't really boho chic. She never had been. She was too preppy for that. And she knew it. Which was why she was schlepping doughnuts and hoping to cultivate some of Adler's more sophisticated bridesmaids as future clients.

She rapped on the door to the suite, and someone Danni didn't know opened it. The woman motioned for her to come in while talking loudly into her phone. The woman nodded toward the other part of the room, and Danni headed over to find the bride and her maid of honor sitting together and chatting.

"Hi," she said, looking for a spot to deposit the doughnuts and coffee thermos before turning back toward them.

"Hey, Danni," Adler said, standing up and coming over to greet her. "You're a lifesaver. This is Iris. Have you two met?"

"Not officially," Iris said. "I love the bracelet you designed for me to wear today."

"Thanks. It's nice to meet you. I feel like I know you because I'm a huge fan of your show," Danni said. "I hope that didn't sound weird. I just meant it's great to meet you in person."

Iris laughed. "It's totally cool. I have done the same thing a million times. Tell me more about your jewelry business."

"Well, I have a few products in stock that I made in bulk and sell from my web shop, but I prefer to do custom work. That's where my main focus is, trying to grow that side of the business. I'm hoping to have a little storefront of my own one day," Danni said.

"I can see where that would be possible. Your designs are really unique, but also the quality is top-notch. When you're ready to open your store, look me up. I'm always interested in investing in women-run businesses. Let me grab one of my business cards," Iris said.

Danni just nodded and stood there while Iris went to her purse and got a card. "Here you go. Can't wait to hear from you."

"Thanks for this," she said, pocketing the card and trying not to get too excited. For all she knew, Iris was just being nice, but Danni couldn't help wanting to squee with joy.

"So what doughnuts did you get for us?"

"They already had a dozen boxed up with Adler's name on it, so I'm not sure what's in here."

Iris opened the box, and a few of the other bridesmaids came over, including the woman who had been on the phone when Danni had arrived.

"Sorry for being so rude earlier," she said by way of introduction. "I was dealing with a catering issue. I mean, it's the wedding day, and the last thing Adler needs is for him to text her about nonsense. I'm Olivia Williams."

"Danni Eldridge."

"Bridesmaid?"

"Jewelry designer. You?"

"Soon to be sister-in-law, bridesmaid and all-around fabu person," Olivia said with a wink. "Actually, I'm also trying to keep everyone calm. Every day there's another bombshell from the parents. Gah, what a messed-up situation."

"You seem totally awesome," Danni said with a return wink. "I'm not up on all the gossip. Figured I'd just keep out of it."

"Good idea," Olivia said. "My mom had an affair with August Bisset. You knew that, right?"

"Yeah, I had heard something about that. But then I heard…it can't be true, but I heard Logan Bisset is actually Nick's twin."

Olivia nodded. "Yeah, that shit's true, too. Adler said if one more revelation comes out today, she's running away, and truth be told, I'm going with her."

"I don't blame you. Surely that's all that is going on between them, right?"

"I hope so. I have been looking forward to having a sister all my life, and I am not letting Adler slip away. So whatever I have to do, I'm going to do it," Olivia said.

Danni liked not only Olivia's attitude but also the love she could hear in the other woman's voice for Adler.

"I've always wanted a sister, too," Adler said, coming over to them. "So I'm happy to get you! Thank you again for bringing these, Danni. I was afraid to go myself because of all the paparazzi trying to snap a photo of me and make a story out of my expression or whatever."

"It really is okay. I can't imagine being in your situation," Danni said.

"Well, to be honest, this isn't the way I thought my wedding day would play out," Adler admitted.

Which made them all start laughing. Danni helped out with hair and makeup where she could but then left the other women to go and get ready for the ceremony herself.

Leo wasn't too sure what to expect when he went down to breakfast. Dare had been chill last night, but he had no idea what he would get from the rest of the family.

Logan looked the worse for wear, as if he'd been

drinking too much or not sleeping. He had a pair of Wayfarer sunglasses on and was sitting at one of the chairs in the middle of the table with a Bloody Mary in front of him.

Normally Leo felt like he was in competition with Logan. A long time ago their gran had said it was natural for younger brothers to feel that way, but Leo wondered if a part of him had sensed that Logan was different, then he immediately dismissed that thought. Logan was his big brother, someone Leo had always looked up to and wanted to be like. As much as Leo had competed to get their father's attention, it was Logan he'd emulated the most.

"Bro, you okay?" he asked, pulling out the chair next to Logan and sitting down.

"Fuck, no," he said. "I haven't talked to Mom, and Dad is mad at me. I made a deal that's going to set Nick and Williams Inc. back, and I know everyone in the family is going to think I'm a dick for doing it. And I have to go to a wedding today and put on my happy face…"

"What deal?"

Logan shoved his hands through his hair. "I bought a patent that Nick has been trying to get for eighteen months and he needs it to move forward with a deal he already had in the works. God, I'm such an asshole sometimes."

"You're not an asshole. You just have to win at all costs. If it helps, Dad is pissed at me, too," Leo said. "Mom will understand, no matter how hurt she might be. She always does. She loves you, Logan. When you are ready, I have no doubt she's going to be right there. Business is business, and Nick knows that better than anyone else. It's not personal, right?"

Logan shrugged and took a sip of his Bloody Mary before he pushed his sunglasses up on his head. "When did you get so smart?"

"I always was, you just never noticed," Leo said. "Seriously, though, no one is going to be looking too closely at you today. So be happy for Adler if you can. This is her day, and I'm pretty sure all eyes will be on her."

"All eyes should be on her," Logan said. "That's the part of all this that really rubs me the wrong way. I mean, I've never made any bones about the fact that I don't like Nick, but even I wouldn't have wanted to see Adler's wedding singed like this."

"Um, what about the patent?"

"That's business."

"Not personal like the parentage thing," Leo said. "No one deserves this kind of situation. Especially not Adler. She's always seemed so strong and able to roll with anything, I guess from bouncing between two worlds like she did. But yesterday...she seemed like she was barely holding herself together."

"Yeah, makes me feel like a douche for having my own feelings."

"She'd be the first to tell you not to beat yourself up over that," Leo said.

"Are you speaking for everyone now?" Logan asked sarcastically.

Leo shook his head. His brother took all the burdens of their family on his shoulders. He got it. They all had a sense of loyalty and guardianship when it came to being Bissets. But in this case, none of this was Logan's fault. "I spent the afternoon with her. We chatted. She doesn't blame you for this, and she even was worried about you. She understands the rivalry between you and Nick probably better than anyone else."

"She does," he said quietly. "I wish I could change things."

"I'm pretty sure you're not the only one," Leo said. "I'm not sure about Dad, though. He probably doesn't think he did anything wrong."

"Or maybe he knows that the past can't be changed, and he has to move forward," their father said from the doorway. He wore a polo shirt and a pair of khaki pants. His salt-and-pepper hair was neatly groomed and his jaw clean-shaven. Leo looked over at his father with a twinge of guilt at what he'd said. But the truth was, Dad hadn't acted as if he felt bad about any of it.

"You should still apologize," Leo said.

"To whom?" Auggie asked.

"Mom, Logan, Nick, Adler…do I need to go on?

Also, what about Dare and me and Zac and Mari?" Leo felt that anger stirring in him again. "You never once made our family your priority, and I get it. I know what it's like to close big deals and watch your profits soar, but until this weekend I had never realized how little you valued us."

"Not everything is about you, Leo," Auggie said. "I'm not answerable to you."

"No, you're not," Leo said. "And to be honest, it doesn't matter anymore. There was a time when I thought you hung the moon. I wanted to follow in your footsteps and have everyone say I was just like you, but not anymore."

He pushed back from the table and stood up.

"Leo. That's enough," Logan said.

"No, it's not. Part of the problem is that no one ever told Dad that he was being an asshole, so he thought it was okay to keep on being one. But not anymore," Leo said. "Sorry if you don't like that."

He walked away from his father and brother and out of the house. He hadn't meant to say any of that, but he hadn't been able to help himself. He knew his father wasn't one to show emotions easily, but he also had never doubted that his father loved him and his siblings. And this weekend he'd realized that he wasn't as sure of that love anymore. Because what man who loved his family would have affairs and father children he didn't know about?

Worse yet was how Leo still wanted to be just like

August. How could he? What was it going to take for him to finally break free of that? He just wished it would happen.

Danni arrived at the wedding ceremony a good forty minutes early. She'd had time to think about Iris's offer, and it made her realize that if she was just herself, she could probably cultivate a few more contacts while she was at the wedding. She was pretty sure Leo would be busy with his family, and after talking to Olivia she got why Leo had needed a distraction the day before. She wasn't even part of their family, and she would have needed more than a distraction if everything she'd ever believed about her siblings and her parents was revealed to be a lie.

She imagined that was going to take him some time to get over, and she knew the last place his mind could be was with her. They'd had some fun, and she was determined to keep that thought firmly in mind.

Then she caught a glimpse of him in his tux standing slightly apart from his brothers. He had on dark sunglasses, and his expression was pensive. He was hotter than she remembered. She wanted to go and try to distract him again.

Except that wasn't her job.

She wasn't his girlfriend. She'd been his Friday-night hookup. That was all.

As tempted as she was to try to make it into something more, she knew better than to lie to herself about him. He wasn't going to suddenly change from his jet-set lifestyle to being a Netflix-and-chill guy. She had to remember that. But it was harder than she wanted it to be.

She saw a few people she recognized as buyers for a large US retail chain. Adler had mentioned that they were going to be here today, and Essie had looked them up on the internet and sent Danni their photos so she could find them. She had a moment where she was torn.

She could do the business thing and go and introduce herself. She had just about convinced herself to do that when she saw Leo turn and walk away from the guests who were milling around on the lawn where the outdoor wedding would take place. She noticed that no one followed him, and she knew it made no sense for her to go after him. Sleeping with Leo wasn't part of her plan for the weekend, yet somehow, he had become that. Somehow, he'd become as important as meeting retail buyers.

She didn't analyze it; she just went right off in the direction where Leo had disappeared. She quickly found him facing the ocean with his hands in his pockets and his head tipped up toward the sun. She stood there for a moment watching him. He was solitary. A man who didn't want or need anyone else around him. She could see that he was conflicted, and to her he seemed…lost.

She knew she couldn't be the one to find him and

bring him back to the wedding in this moment. He wasn't physically lost, he was spiritually lost, and she recognized that because she had been the same way for so long until she'd decided to quit practicing law and turn her Etsy shop into a profit-making business. Which was why she should be talking to those buyers so she wouldn't have to go back to the law practice. But she was here.

Because this man called to her in a way that she struggled to understand. She didn't want to be standing here watching him. Aching for him. Witnessing his pain over the fact that the father he loved and looked up to wasn't the man Leo had always believed him to be.

"Want some company?" she asked, feeling like she had to say something. If she kept staring at him, she was going to start trying to convince herself that all sorts of things about him were true.

"Not sure how good I'll be, but yes," he said, glancing over his shoulder at her. "Damn, you look good."

She smiled at the way he said it. "Thanks. Figured I couldn't just show up with my hair blowing around me like a storm."

"I would have liked it," he said. "You try too hard to be this buttoned-up version of yourself. I like it when you are wild and free."

She'd come out here to help him, to bring him back to the fold, but he was looking at her, looking past the barriers she'd put up and dropping truth bombs she wasn't ready to deal with. She did try hard to be the woman she wanted the world to see, but she wasn't sure if that was who *she* truly wanted to be.

"I like you when you smile," she said, ignoring his remark as best she could. "But you're not today."

"Yeah. I keep saying things that I shouldn't. Keep getting angry with my family. I wasn't kidding when I said I'm bad company today."

She walked over and stood next to him. "You might be, but you were smart enough to remove yourself from them for a little while. Was it something about your brother?"

"Logan?"

"Yes. You two seemed awfully close yesterday. I hope you still are."

"We are," he said. "I'm not mad at Logan. I'm mad at my parents, and a part of me knows that I shouldn't be. I'm not the child most affected by their deceit, yet I am still hurting. I can't help it. I want them both to realize that they have shattered what our family was, and I'm not sure I can go back to being the loyal son I was before."

She had no way to help him through this. No words that would ease his conscience or make him feel okay. So she did the one thing that her gut told her to do. She put her arm around his waist. He stood there stiffly for a moment before he put his arm around her shoulder and hugged her to his side.

He didn't say anything else and neither did she until the wedding coordinator came to get him because the wedding was about to begin.

Ten

Leo wasn't surprised when his mom pulled him aside after the ceremony while the photographer was taking photos of different groups. As soon as she was done being photographed with Adler, Juliette looped her arm through his and walked him away from the rest of the family.

"Mom, this isn't the time," he said, having an idea that he was going to be getting a talk, which was how his mom had always referred to any type of discipline she had to mete out to them when they were children.

"It's the perfect time, Lion. We don't have to be

at the reception for thirty minutes or so, and I think you need someone to talk to."

"Not you, Mom," he said. "I don't want to say any of the things that are in my head to you."

She stopped near some of the seats that were still set up from the service and gestured for him to sit down. He did, and she sat next to him. Putting her arm on the back of his chair, she turned so that her knees were facing toward him, and he did the same. Looking into her pretty eyes, he couldn't help but remember all the times in his life that he'd come to her for comfort and advice. All the times he'd just turned to her knowing she'd be the solid rock of the Bisset family.

And for the first time when he looked at her, he wasn't just seeing the love that he always saw in her expression. He saw her pain, too. This was what he'd wanted to avoid. He didn't want to be his asshole self with his mom. She was already tearing herself up with guilt and recriminations. He knew she didn't need to hear it from him. God knew how she was going to deal with Logan.

"Lion, if you don't say it, then we can't move past it. I know what I did was wrong and that it has really had a profound effect on the family. I also heard what you said to your father...thank you for defending me, but the blame for my deceit is mine and mine alone. You know I believe that we are all responsible for our actions," she said.

He did know that. Many times when he was younger, he'd tried to defend doing something he knew she wouldn't approve of by using the justification that Logan or Dare had done something worse. That argument had never worked on her. "I know that. But at the same time, you're the one who always was home with us and loving us… I can't blame you for this, Mom, not that it's even my right to place blame. I guess what I'm saying is I don't want to direct the anger I feel at you. I hate that the family we had was a lie, and I'm trying to sort out where that leaves me. I've always been so proud of our family— even our arrogance. I thought that was okay because we were good people."

She didn't say anything in response, and he wondered if he'd gone too far. Then he got mad at himself and her. She'd been the one to force this conversation when he hadn't wanted it. He should have dashed out of the photo session to go find Danni. She was just the excuse he could use to get away from this.

"We are still good people. Good people aren't perfect, Leo, and I'll thank you to remember that everyone makes mistakes. I was trying to do the right thing, and once I took that action, I had no other option but to stick with my lie. You've made mistakes, as well," she said. "Your father and I have a complicated relationship, but the one thing that even you have to admit is that we have always loved you and your siblings."

She was right, but then, she knew she was. He stood up. "I know that. This is why I didn't want to talk. I'm not ready to be a grown-up about this yet. I feel like all of my life has been a lie, and I have to figure out how to get past it. There is nothing that's going to magically make this okay, which I think you know. I love you, Mom, but I need time to get over being mad at Dad and, in some small way, you."

She stood up, as well. "Fair enough."

She stood so straight, her pride lending her the illusion of being taller than she already was. He put his arms around her and hugged her close. "I love you."

She hugged him back, and for a minute it felt like everything would be okay in their world. He stepped back and moved away from her. "I'll see you later at the reception."

"See you there."

He walked away, knowing that his other siblings and the Williams family were probably watching him. A part of him knew that he needed to reel in his emotions, but for the first time in his life, his path was broken. It wasn't that he couldn't see it—it was that something impassable had grown up in front of him and the way forward was barred. He had no idea what to do next.

And it wasn't business that had him flummoxed, it was his personal life. He had Danni, who had been a breath of fresh air and comfort when he needed it, but he had no idea where that was going. If anywhere.

She wasn't looking for anything with him, and he was leaving his family and racing to be by her side. Did that mean as much as it seemed to?

Or was she just an escape?

He didn't want to use her and would hate himself if he did that. But at the same time, he wasn't going to let this bring him to his knees, and he would use whatever—or whoever—he needed to in order to get his mojo back.

Danni enjoyed the wedding more than she'd expected to. After knowing all that Adler and Nick had been through in the last three days, Danni had cried when they'd looked into each other's eyes and said, "I do." It was a special moment that had made Danni realize that once she got her business off the ground, she wanted to find a man who looked at her the way Nick had looked at Adler.

She had been seated in the same row with some of Marielle's influencer friends, and they were nice and friendly but had immediately left to post videos and photos from the event. Danni stood off to one side trying to observe them, but she was distracted, watching as Leo and his family posed for their photos with Adler and Nick and then with Adler and her dad.

And one thing that Danni observed was how they all smiled. They were really good at looking happy and like everything was perfect for the photographer.

Her family would have all been glaring at each other if they were having the kind of weekend the Bissets were. As soon as the photographer was done with them and they were dismissed, Leo started to walk away, but his mom caught up to him and drew him off to the side for a private conversation.

Danni watched for a moment before realizing what she was doing. It wasn't any of her business. She needed to get herself to the reception and start schmoozing like the other guests instead of watching Leo.

But again, she felt that pull toward him. It wasn't just sexual. Of course, she wasn't denying that he was hot, and she had thought about their time together at odd moments during the day—especially when the minister had said Nick could kiss the bride. She'd had this weird little vision of herself as the bride getting kissed by Leo...

But that wasn't going to happen. He wasn't the marrying kind, especially after the huge mistakes his parents had made. To be honest, it was enough to make her think twice about marriage.

"Hey, you on your own?"

She glanced over to see Olivia Williams walking toward her, swinging her bridesmaid bouquet in one hand. "Yes. I guess I should have brought a plus-one, but I figured I'd be working."

"But now you wish you had? It's so awkward when you're doing a social event for business. Happens to me all the time. Dad tends to make one of my brothers go with me but that's even more annoying, because then they are trying to ditch me so they can find someone to—"

"Someone to what, Liv? Are you going to deny that you ditched me the last time to hook up with Beau Montrose?"

The guy who came up and put his arm over Olivia's shoulder bore a strong resemblance to her. But for the life of her, Danni couldn't remember the name of any of her brothers except Nick, and that was because he was the groom.

"Why shouldn't she do that?" Danni asked.

"Good point, Ash. You've done it often enough," Olivia said.

He put his hands up. "I was trying to say there was equal dumping going on. I'm Asher, by the way, and you are?"

"Danni Eldridge."

"Nice to meet you," he said, holding out his hand, which she shook and let drop. "Are we heading over to the reception?"

"Yes, Danni's going to join us. She's stagging it," Olivia said.

"Are you looking for a—"

"Stop now," Olivia interrupted him. "She's not interested in you."

"Liv, we don't know that for sure," Asher said. The two of them cracked Danni up. It was clear to see they had a close relationship. She envied it, having never really been that close to her siblings.

It was different than the way Logan and Leo had interacted but just as sincere and solid.

"She's right. I'm kind of seeing someone," Danni said. It felt odd to mention it. It wasn't like she and Leo had solid plans. But she wasn't going to pretend that he didn't exist.

"Of course you are. You are too lovely to be on your own," Ash said.

"Stop it before I gag. Do you ever get a girl to go home with you?" Olivia said.

"Women like a guy who treats them with kindness, Liv. Also, they don't like to be called girls."

Olivia rolled her eyes as she looked over at Danni. "He's so woke."

"I am," Ash said. "Come on, ladies, I'll escort you to the reception."

He held out each of his arms. Olivia looped her arm through his left and Danni was reaching for the right when someone slipped his arm through hers first.

"I'll escort Danni," Leo said.

She looked up at him. His expression was inscrutable and fierce. Ash just nodded. "That's cool. She was standing all alone, and that's never comfortable at a wedding."

"That's true. Thanks for being a gentleman," Leo said.

"Uh, before you two start patting yourselves on the back, Danni and I were taking care of ourselves just fine," Olivia stated.

"Of course you were. That's not what we were saying," Ash said. "Come on, Liv, let's go."

Danni watched them walk away. "I didn't know if I should wait for you or what."

"I know. I haven't been the best guy to be around today. But when I saw you with them... I want you with me, Danni. I want to enjoy the party and pretend that I don't have to deal with the messes I've made. Just for a few hours. What do you say?"

She wanted to just say yes. But he had no idea how complicated he was. How much he was pulling at her in so many different ways. She wanted to figure out a way to fix him but knew she never could. But for a few hours...

"Yes."

The reception was fun. The band was good. Toby Osborn sang a song to Adler for her first dance with Nick that made everyone cry. Then he did a set of his hits to get everyone dancing. All in all, Leo was finding Danni made it very easy for him to shove all the messy stuff with his family aside. He drank the signature cocktail, a blackberry whiskey lemonade that went down very easily, and Danni kept pace with him.

They danced and laughed a lot. She looked perplexed a time or two, as if she wasn't sure why he was dancing just with her, and he could have told her it was because she was the only woman he had eyes for. But he knew that was the alcohol talking. Yet it wasn't just the drinks that made him possessive of her and want to express feelings he knew he needed to keep to himself.

When Toby and his band played the opening chords of "Brown-Eyed Girl," Danni leaped to her feet. "This is my song. You have to dance with me."

He threw back the rest of his drink and grabbed her hand, leading her out onto the dance floor. They walked by the Williams family, and Danni saw Olivia in the group.

"Girl, this is our song," Danni yelled over to her. "Yaas!"

Leo wasn't sure how, but he found himself dancing in a group with Danni, Olivia, Asher, his brother Zac and Zac's girlfriend, Iris. Somehow it made sense to stay on the dance floor for the next few songs, and when the band slowed to "Tenerife Sea" by Ed Sheeran, he pulled Danni close.

She was supple and pliant, her body fitting into the curves of his as she wrapped her arms around him. She ran her fingers against the back of his neck as she sang the words she knew—every other one—and closed her eyes, resting her head against his shoulder. He wanted this moment to last forever.

They weren't in love, but right now he felt like

they could be. That he could be a different man. He held her as the music played, and even with everyone swaying around them, it felt like it was just the two of them. He could be the man she needed him to be. But hell, he wasn't even sure she was looking for a man.

He'd never been one to put a woman first. Not like this. Not like he was feeling it in this moment. He danced her to the edge of the dance floor and then took her hand and led her outside until they were alone under the clear moonlit sky.

The music could still be heard in the distance, and she looked up at him with those wide, kind eyes, her trusting heart in them.

God, she should never look at him like that.

He was feeling so many things. He wanted to remind himself that tomorrow he might once again consider her a distraction, but tonight...tonight she was everything he needed.

He didn't want to think about anything else in the world except Danni and how she looked tonight. Her hair was curling a little more wildly around her face than it had during the wedding ceremony.

Her eyes sparkled with the passion and intelligence that he realized she brought to everything she did. When her full lips fell into an easy smile, he admitted to himself he couldn't resist wanting to kiss her.

"Why did you bring us out here?" she asked.

"I wanted to kiss you," he said. "And there are too many people in that room for the kind of kiss I want."

"Are you going to ask my permission again?" she teased.

He groaned.

"No," he said. He was a goner where she was concerned.

He lowered his mouth and kissed her. She opened her lips under his, and her tongue rubbed over his as she held on to his shoulders and went up on her tiptoes to deepen the kiss even more.

She tasted of blackberries and whiskey and Danni. Something so uniquely her that he knew he'd never forget it.

He pulled back. She was still on her tiptoes. The skirt of her organza dress swirled around them when he lifted her off her feet and kissed her again. He knew he was running from something and that kissing her was the path he'd chosen.

This kiss was going to take him away from the family complications he'd left behind at the reception. Now he was on a path that his gut wasn't sure was going to lead anywhere. But he knew he wouldn't be steered away from her.

"Want to go back to your place?" he asked. "I'm staying with my entire family at my gran's cottage and that could make the morning awkward. Also I've had enough of the party and I just want you."

His words sounded raw when he said them, and

he wondered if she could feel the need in him. He hoped she didn't sense how much he was craving her and needing her in this moment. He didn't want her to see that.

"Yes. Let me get my bag from inside and we can go," she said.

She took his hand in hers, and they walked back into the reception, bumping into a couple who were leaving. He looked up into his father's eyes, then saw that August was holding his mom's hand.

"Good night, son. Hope you had a nice evening," his dad said.

"Dad." He nodded his head. "Good night."

Leo started to move by them, but his mom reached out and hugged him. "Love you, son."

He nodded. And Danni tugged her hand free. "I'll grab my purse while you say good night."

He let her go but then stood awkwardly next to his parents. The cocktails and his regret and anger all mixed together. "I'm sorry I've been so vocal about things."

"You wouldn't be our son if you weren't," his dad said.

And Leo realized that he *was* their son. No matter what else he might feel, he was always going to be the best and worst of his parents.

Eleven

Leo was a little bit drunk, and it was funny to see the normally buttoned-up, intense man so relaxed. He took her hand as they left the reception at the Nantucket Hotel and walked toward the cottage she'd rented for the week.

"Did you see my parents?" he asked.

"I did," she said. "They seemed pretty solid despite all the gossip about them. You were right about your dad. He kind of draws all the attention in the room."

"Yeah, I guess they are. I've been a jerk to both of them," Leo said. "It's so hard to stop seeing my mom and dad from a kid's perspective. From how I saw them growing up. I mean, I know they are adults who have another life entirely, but still…"

"I think that's always the way of the parent-child relationship. We see our parents' choices in terms of how they affect us. We don't really see how they're making the only decision they can for themselves and what they think was right for you."

He took her hand and tugged her into his arms, kissing her lightly. "You're really smart."

"Thanks," she said. Knowing she was just of average intelligence but hadn't downed as many cocktails as Leo, she probably seemed smarter to him at this moment.

"And pretty. And sexy. Why are you single?"

"Because I'm a modern woman who isn't defined by being in a relationship," she said. She'd had a lot of time to practice that answer, because she got asked the question a lot. She had goals and things she wanted to accomplish and, yes, at some point, she wanted to find a man to share her life with, but right now she had other things going on. Something that Leo had complicated this weekend.

He dropped her hand and put his up in surrender. "I was just asking. Seems like some guy would have snatched you up by now."

"I guess I'm not as great in the everyday," she said. "Why are you single?"

"It's my brand and my parents have had a very tumultuous and complicated relationship, so that example is always one I wanted to avoid following. I want to be successful and don't want to be absent the way my dad was."

She thought about what he said. It was funny how the older she got, the more she realized that her parents were the driving force in everything she thought she had to do and that she felt like a rebel when she did the things she wanted to.

"Good thing we're both single then," she said.

"Definitely good. We wouldn't have had last night or tonight together," he said.

And that was it, she told herself firmly. Tonight was going to be it. Tomorrow after the brunch to celebrate Nick and Adler, she was supposed to head back home, and Leo was going back to his life on Long Island. Which was how it should be.

"Where do you live?" he asked. "I don't know anything about your real life."

"I live in Boston, in one of the suburbs there," she said.

"Own your own home?"

"As a matter of fact, I do," she said. "My parents cosigned the loan. They have a thing about rent being a waste of money."

"Good point, and property is always a good investment. I own my own home, too," he said.

"Yeah, I know. I've seen the Leo Bisset Clubhouse photos on your social. Your place looks so dreamy and perfect. I always want to curl up on the chair by the fireplace."

He had used his elegant home as the setting for many of his ads and he decorated it with the items he was selling. He'd somehow managed to tap into the zeitgeist and created a home that appealed to many people and made them want to try to recreate it for themselves.

"Yeah? You'll have to come and visit some time. It's really comfy and seats two easily," he said.

She knew she wasn't going to visit him. He was drunk, offering something that wasn't going to happen. A minute before, they'd said this night would be their last together. Yet here he was mentioning something else… Which was his real desire? And which was hers?

Most of the time she was on her own through her own conscious decision to steer clear of men who wanted more. Yet with Leo she was torn. He could be so beneficial to her business with his knowledge and skills. But time after time, she found herself doing this instead of picking his brain. She preferred holding his hand and talking to him about life things.

Where was her focus?

Why couldn't she put Leo back in the box of hot hookup, instead of whatever this was?

She didn't like the answer circling around in her mind, so she shoved it away. She wasn't falling for him. He wasn't her kind of guy. He was too business-

focused and not himself because of the scandal rock-
ing his family. He'd needed her this weekend. But in
the real world, he wouldn't need her at all.

Remember that.

But when they got to her cottage, he pulled her
into his arms and she started to lose her resolve.
"This night was about the best one I've had in a long
time. Thanks to you."

He lowered his head and kissed her. Just a soft,
gentle kiss as his hands fell to her waist and he held
her lightly next to him. His tongue made languid
strokes into her mouth, igniting a fire deep inside
her.

She put her hands around his shoulders and kissed
him back. She wasn't going to dwell on anything but
Leo tonight. This Leo, the one who was with her, not
the one he was going to be on Monday when they
were back in the real world.

He was her perfect wedding date, and she was
going to enjoy every second she had with him. Every
brush of his mouth over hers. Every caress of his
hands on her skin. Every single passionate moment
that she could wring from this night.

She wanted it and wasn't going to hesitate to take
it. She needed him, and it seemed he needed her. She
realized that being with him had awakened something inside her that she'd ignored for too long.

He made her want to be more than the boss babe
she was always aiming to be. She wanted to be a

complete woman. Not that he completed her, but he made her realize that by ignoring this passionate side of herself, she wasn't being true to the woman she was.

Leo found the night air refreshing, and being with Danni brought out his Zen side…well, maybe not really, but right now he didn't feel that anger that had been his constant companion throughout the day as his family had been forced to smile and act as if everything was okay.

With Danni he'd just let all that fall to the wayside. He thought it was probably because she tasted so damn good when he kissed her. Or maybe it was because she dressed with such elegance and grace, but her body was pure temptation. Or maybe it was… Ah, hell, he thought, who really cared?

He had Danni in his arms, and he was going to take complete advantage of the fact that she was letting him back into her bed. One last night. It was just what he needed so that when he looked back on Adler's wedding it would be with fondness instead of that murky bitterness that everything else had stirred.

"Want to come inside?" she asked. "Or were you planning on kissing me on the lawn all night long?"

He leaned back from her, looking down at her heart-shaped face with a tendril of hair curling over her cheek. "You are the sassiest woman."

She lifted both eyebrows, and her eyes seemed to sparkle. "Thanks. So, are you coming in?"

"Oh, I definitely am. I don't think anything could make me leave you alone tonight," he said, lifting her off her feet and swinging her up in his arms as he carried her to the front door.

She put one arm around his shoulders to brace herself. When he got to the front door, he set her on her feet, and she pulled her key from her purse. She opened the door, and he followed her into the hallway of the cottage. She tossed her purse on the table as she turned to face him, her face illuminated by a light left on in the main living area.

He reached up and took off his tie, putting it on the table next to her bag. She kicked off her heels, and he toed off his shoes and then his socks. She glanced down at his bare feet, then back up at his face. "Only you could look sophisticated with no shoes on."

"Oh, I think you could give me a run for my money," he said. She looked to him, as she always did. Somehow too good for the jaded world he lived in.

He knew from the moment they met that she was different, and each minute he'd spent with her just reinforced it. She held her hand out.

He took it, and she led him down the hall to the bedroom. He saw her open, partially packed suitcase on the end of the bed as she flicked on the light. The reminder was stark. She was leaving tomorrow. She'd be back to her old life, and he'd be back to his.

Back to creating products that promised a dream that millions aspired to have in their own life while knowing how hollow and fake those picturesque images really were.

"Sorry about the mess. I didn't expect…"

"To bring me back here?"

"Yeah," she said, moving around him to close her suitcase and take it off the bed. She put it in the corner and then turned back to him, and he smiled at her.

"I wasn't expecting it, either, but I'm very glad I'm here," he said. He sometimes felt that he didn't say the right thing when he should, and with Danni he wanted to give her all the words he usually kept tucked away.

"Me, too," she said.

But she was standing there awkwardly, looking like she didn't know what to do next. He realized that there had been too much time since that fiery kiss in her front yard, and she was slowly coming back down from the wedding reception haze.

"Do you still want me here?" he asked.

"More than anything," she admitted.

"Me, too," he said. "But I think we need a dance

or something to get us back to where we were. Suggestions?"

"You could strip for me," she said, blushing only the tiniest bit as she said it.

"Strip for you?" he asked. No one had ever asked him to do that. He'd had a few women do a striptease for him before, but he'd never been the one… "Okay. But only if you are naked on the bed watching me."

"Fair enough," she said. She reached for the side of her dress, drew the zipper down and then lifted the dress up over her head. Now she was standing there in just a tiny pair of lacy panties and some kind of strapless bra.

She walked over to the bed, piled up the pillows, and as she leaned over, he couldn't help but groan at the shape of her ass. She had curvy hips and shapely legs. He remembered how good they had felt when she'd straddled him on the yacht.

She glanced over her shoulder at him. Then she straightened and removed the bra and slowly worked her panties down her legs, stepping out of them before climbing up on the bed. She rested her back against the pile of pillows. Her legs were slightly parted, and she draped her arms out to her sides.

"I'm ready."

"So am I," he said. But he wasn't sure he was ready for Danni. Not for anything more than a night of sexual fun—and that's all this was. Why, then, did something in his soul crave more?

* * *

Leo's expression was inscrutable, and as she'd never been to a strip club, she wasn't sure what she was expecting. But he took his time, slowly unbuttoning his dress shirt to reveal his tanned, lithe body. He had an innate sensuality in all his moves, and as he took off his clothes for her, his gaze captured hers and she felt her temperature rising. She was already turned on from a night of dancing and laughing.

She realized that when she was with Leo, she felt like she was the woman she wanted to be. A part of her was afraid she was just pretending but another part believed that they had connected on a different level. A deeper level than either of them really wanted.

She felt her breasts getting heavier as she got moist between her thighs. He took his shirt off and tossed it toward the chair next to the window. Then he turned and put his hands on his waist, and she caught her breath as she realized how hard he was. His pants weren't hiding his erection, and she sat up and held her arm out, beckoning him to her with the crook of her finger.

"Not yet, baby. I'm not done giving you the show you asked for," he said.

"I can't wait to see everything," she said.

He undid his pants and swiveled his hips as he lowered them. They fell down his thighs to his ankles, and he stepped out of them. He wore a pair of tight-fitting boxer briefs that hugged his package, and she shifted forward again, getting on her hands and knees and crawling across the mattress to the side of the bed where he was standing.

"I'll do the last part."

She didn't wait for him to say yes or no, just took the elastic waistband in her hands and shoved his underwear down, careful to maneuver it over his erection. Once his boxer briefs were down to his thighs, she took his hard-on in her hand. He was bigger than she remembered, and harder. She stroked him up and down, leaning forward to take the tip of him into her mouth. He groaned, his hands falling to the back of her head, urging her to take more of him in her mouth, which she did. She sucked on him until he pulled away and urged her to lie back on the bed. He then eased himself up her body, letting his entire torso caress her as he did so.

His mouth was hot and heavy on hers, the kiss deep and dark with sexual promises that she would make sure he kept. She wanted everything he had to give her.

He shifted his shoulders, his chest hair abrading her sensitive nipples. Feeling the tip of his erection at the entrance to her body, she parted her thighs farther and wrapped one of her legs around his hips as he drove himself into her.

She closed her eyes, wrapping her arms around his shoulders. His mouth was on hers, sucking her tongue deeper into his mouth as he drove into her with a strong rhythm that pushed her toward her climax. She felt it just there, out of her reach, but then he rubbed her clit with his thumb, as he thrust deep in her and she tightened around him, arching her back as her climax rolled through her.

He groaned—a rough, guttural sound that rumbled through his entire body. Cupping her butt in his palm, he drove into her at an even faster pace, pushing her toward a second climax. She clung to him, threw her head back and cried out his name as she came again. She was losing all control, but she didn't care. She felt him come just after her and held him to her as he continued to thrust a couple more times, causing another tiny orgasm to ripple through her.

She fell back against the bed; his head dropped to her shoulder, and he kept his weight off her with his arms and legs. She opened her eyes a few minutes later to find him watching her, and there was an expression on his face that she couldn't define. She didn't even try to, because she didn't want to risk thinking this was anything more than these few carefree nights on Nantucket.

"I think you should know that if your business fails, you would probably be able to strip for a living," she finally said, breaking the silence.

That surprised a bark of laughter from him. It made her happy to see him laugh, but another part of her wondered why she'd done that. Why she'd deflected her fears with a joke, to make light of a deeper emotion that she was still feeling all the way inside. Because this was definitely more than sex, as much as she was afraid to admit it to herself.

"Woman, you are a constant surprise," he said as he rolled to his side and took her with him.

She cuddled against him but felt dampness on her legs and knew she should get up and clean up. But at the same time, she knew that she had only a few more opportunities to be curled in his arms. To hear his heartbeat beneath her ear and feel his hand languidly caressing her back. She looked up as she felt a tug on one of her curls and saw he was winding it around his finger, looking down at it like… like he was lost.

She knew he was.

That was why this was just for the weekend. Just a wedding fling, nothing more. It couldn't be, because she had stuff she needed to do, and no matter how much her soft heart wanted to add saving Leo to the agenda, there wasn't room for that. Not mentally or emotionally.

Twelve

Waking up a married woman was nothing like Adler had expected. Nick was snoring, as he'd had too much to drink the night before, and she had a champagne headache. Not sexy, not glam, not at all how she'd thought they'd start their life together. But that was par for the course.

They were scheduled to have a brunch with their friends and family later this morning, and they could both deal with everything that had come up over the last few days. It was so hard to remember how excited she'd been about becoming a bride just a few short days ago, before all the scandal hit. Life had felt…so full of promise.

"Adler?"

She glanced over at Nick. He'd rolled to his side and was watching her. He was so handsome, with his square jaw and brown eyes that always seemed so bright in his dark face. He had a bit of stubble on his jaw, but to be honest, he didn't really look the worse for wear after all his drinking the night before.

"Husband?" she said back. A lot of stuff had gone on between the two of them this weekend, and she wanted their first day as husband and wife to set a new tone. All that crap from the Bissets wasn't going to have a negative impact on her life. She wasn't going to let it.

"Wife," he said, pulling her into his arms and hugging her tightly to him. "That sounds good. I'm sorry for how crazy my behavior has been over the last few days. It's just been a lot and if I didn't have you by my side I think I might have lost it."

She hugged him back. "It's okay. How are you feeling today?"

"Surprisingly good. I know there's still crap to deal with in terms of August and my mom, but last night was nice. And ultimately, though I think that our two families aren't ever going to be friends, they can at least be cordial."

"Good," she said. "I don't even know what you're going to do with August. But my cousins are all decent—it's still hard to believe they're your half siblings."

"I know. I still hate Logan, and now I come to find out he's my twin. How is that even possible?" Nick said.

"Yeah, it's a mess. But we are leaving for Fiji tonight, and we can have two weeks away from the world. Will you be okay with that?"

"Yes. I need it. I want to get back to us instead of focusing on this stuff. It never really bothered me that I didn't know who my biological father was, you know? I have my dad and he's always been one hundred percent that man for me. I wasn't missing anything, and my family felt complete. So, learning that someone like August was my biological father was hard to handle."

"I bet. He's been my auntie's husband all my life, but I've never really had a close bond with him. He's sort of all about business and making sure that the world knows that the Bissets are on top."

"Yeah, Dad hates that about him."

She nodded. She didn't want to be talking about her uncle the morning after her wedding, but he was Nick's biological father and he'd been so quiet about it up until this point. She knew he'd been shaken and he'd been dealing with it by drinking too much, but otherwise he'd kept it all locked in until she'd pushed him to show her what he was feeling. That's what being married was about.

"You do, too," she said. "I guess you aren't going

to suddenly have a father-son relationship with him, are you?"

"You know, he hasn't even tried to talk to me," Nick said. "So I guess not. I'm more concerned about Logan. I think… I'd like to get to know him better. He seemed open to that, as well. He offered to give me the patent he stole as a wedding present. Maybe I can find a way to make that work."

"I'm pretty good friends with Quinn, and she and Logan seem to be an item again now. We can all do a dinner party after we're back from our honeymoon," she said. "I can help you navigate that if you want."

"Yeah, that might be the way to do it," Nick said. "I don't want it to affect our business. I mean, I'm not proposing a merger or going softer on Bisset Industries now that we are related. I still don't really feel that we're family, you know?"

She nodded and realized that this was the conversation she wished they could have been having all along instead of dodging the paparazzi and trying to deal with the scandal through the media instead of with each other. Part of her nerves, she knew, came from the fact that everyone who wanted to could know her business. She'd always hated that part of growing up in the spotlight.

"I get it. And besides all of that, we are family now. We are starting our own little Williams clan, and I don't want any of that scandal to touch us."

"I can't promise it won't, but I'll do my best to

keep it away from us," he said. "I don't want to spend my life living a lie with you. That was one thing I thought about a lot. How Auggie and my mom's affair had led to all of this…and then your aunt Juliette…"

"I know. I was shocked to hear she'd do something like that. But she always has been the kind of woman to do whatever was needed to do. She's been a surrogate mom to me, so I know how much she loves all of her kids. She never treated Logan any different."

"I thought so. She was welcoming to me from the first, even though she knew my family and the Bissets had this business rivalry. She's a gracious lady. This has to have been hard on her."

"I think so, too," Adler said, knowing that her aunt had done her best to make this wedding perfect for her but at the same time had struggled with her own guilt over her part in the scandal. "Your mom, too. Who would have thought those two would be at the heart of this?"

"Not me," Nick said. "I'll be glad to get the brunch over and have you to myself."

"Can't wait," Adler said.

Danni woke to the smell of coffee and Leo sitting on the edge of the bed, dressed in a polo shirt and khakis. She wasn't sure when he'd had time to go get a change of clothes. She pulled the bedsheets with her as she sat up.

"Good morning, gorgeous," he said as he handed her the steaming mug.

She took it from him, pushing her hair off her face, and then panicked as she realized her curls were probably doing their normal Medusa-morning thing. She reached up to try to pat them into place with one hand, but Leo caught her wrist and drew her hand down.

"Don't touch it. I love your hair all wild and free," he said. "You seem to spend most of your waking hours taming it, and I wonder if you aren't taming yourself, too."

She wasn't sure she was ready for this much honesty on a Sunday morning. She took a sip of coffee and then leaned back to study him. "Feeling philosophical?"

"Yeah. That, and I don't want to leave you with the impression that I was just a big ball of anger and rage."

"And sexy stripteases," she said, trying to keep it light. But her throat was tight. He was saying goodbye. He was right to do it now, before they saw each other again in public. She knew that, but she wasn't ready. She had just woken up. She hadn't had time to tame her crazy hair or reel in the emotions she wasn't going to acknowledge she had. She still needed to lock them away before she could deal with this conversation.

"Yeah, that…no one would believe you if you told them," he said.

"Seriously, you were fun. A bit of a complication that I wasn't anticipating, but given the impression I had of you, you were much better than I thought you'd be," she admitted. He had been human, which sounded silly when she said it in her head, but the truth was, he had seemed like a cardboard man until they'd first met and played golf together at the scramble.

"I like that. I wasn't sure why you were with me," he said. "The novelty of being with a Bisset or something else?"

She was taken aback by that. "I don't care that you are a Bisset. I think your family puts too much stock in your name."

She knew her words were harsh but didn't really care. What he'd just said wasn't very nice, either.

"You're right about that. I didn't mean it the way you took it. I was just trying to figure us out."

"You're hot. Apparently, you thought I was, too, and we hooked up, Leo," she said, feeling a little mad that he'd taken the conversation in this direction. "That's all it was."

He nodded, but his jaw was tighter. "I guess that is all. You seemed like a woman who would need more than heat to sleep with a guy," he said at last.

"Maybe I thought you were a different sort of guy, or maybe you're not as smart about me as you think you are," she said. "But that doesn't matter. Thanks for the coffee."

She wasn't sure how to ask him to leave. She was lying naked in the bed where he'd made love to her the night before. She'd thought she was storing memories for the future, but he was plotting how to make his escape.

"You're welcome. I phoned up to my grandmother's house and asked Michael to bring breakfast with my change of clothes. How about if I leave you to your coffee and wait in the other room? We can have breakfast together, if that works for you."

"Sure," she said.

"I think I upset you," he said. "I'm sorry. I'm still not in my right mind after everything that's happened with my family this weekend."

She softened toward him but then realized what she was doing and just forced a smile instead. He was projecting his wounded feelings onto her, and she was allowing it. But she needed to stop, because that kind of bond didn't really exist between them.

He'd been upset and needed a distraction during the wedding, and she'd been there waiting for something from him that he couldn't give her.

"You're fine. Will breakfast keep if I take a quick shower?" she asked.

"Yes. Michael brought the ingredients and instructions. Your fridge was empty," he said.

"I know. Okay, give me fifteen minutes," she said.

He got up and stood there as if he had something more to say, but then he just turned and walked out of the bedroom. She braced herself for the rest of the morning and everything he'd set in motion. He was walking out of her life—he'd made that clear. If there was any lingering hope from the night before, it was time to kill it.

Leo had been trying to be a good guy, not like his usual self—or like his father—but he knew it had backfired. He wasn't super in touch with his feelings and would never think of himself as having a good read on women, but he could tell he'd pissed Danni off. He was a second away from texting Dare and asking him for advice. But this wasn't a relationship. He'd been trying to give them some closure before they both had to get on the ferry and go home. Though first, he was taking a helicopter to Martha's Vineyard for a photo shoot with Tommy Hilfiger for a partnership he'd worked on.

And he realized after watching his dad's past affair bite him in the ass that Leo didn't want any surprises years from now. He should have used a condom, even though Danni had said she was on the pill. But this weekend he'd been shaken, and it had made him stupid.

Danni seemed like this wild, ethereal woman, but he remembered when they first met she'd definitely had an agenda. Somewhere along the way, as he'd been rocked by the revelation of his parents' secrets, he'd forgotten all that and let himself fall for Danni. He needed to get them back on track. Fix this, make sure she knew if anything resulted from their nights together, he wanted to know now, not thirty years from now.

He heard the shower shut off and looked at the instructions that Michael had written for him. The breakfast casserole he'd brought for Leo to fix was already partially baked and needed to be reheated for fifteen minutes, so Leo put it in the oven. Michael had set the table on the back porch for them, complete with a bottle of champagne in an ice bucket and a chilled pitcher of fresh-squeezed orange juice.

Everything was perfect, the way his grandmother's butler always did things. Leo knew that the only thing messing up the morning was him. He wasn't sure why. It wasn't as if this was a first for him; he'd done this before. He'd slept with plenty of women then said goodbye. But this was Danni, and she'd seen him in a more vulnerable state than anyone else. And now he regretted that.

He should never have revealed so much of himself to her. He should have kept his guard up. But he hadn't been able to. He'd been reeling and falling, and he'd landed in her soft arms.

He looked around the tiny kitchen while he waited for her to finish getting ready and saw some notes she'd jotted down. They were all about partnering with brands and meeting buyers.

He remembered how she'd asked him about keeping their relationship business-focused. She'd wanted something from him, and he was pretty sure he hadn't delivered anything other than some hot nights.

Her list was small, and he knew she'd have to broaden her goals if she was going to make it big. She was taking tiny risks, and so her results would be smaller. He jotted a few things on the paper underneath each of her topics. Just advice that would help her.

At the bottom he wrote, *You have to stop being timid and asking politely for what you want. Take it, Danni, and you will get more than you realized was out there.*

He put the pen down as he heard the bedroom door open. Danni walked out, dressed in a pair of white slacks and a floral blouse with a bow at the neck. She had her hair pulled back in a low bun, and her makeup was flawless. He knew he was seeing Danni Eldridge, businesswoman, not the Danni he'd been with all weekend.

And somehow, as much as her appearance signaled that she'd gotten his message, a small part of him was disappointed. Did he want her to beg him to stay? To keep seeing each other after they went home?

No, he scoffed. He wasn't in the market for a serious girlfriend, and if he was, Danni didn't fit his image. She was too real and solid. And that worried him. He wasn't what she needed. She had that earnest authenticity that he could never achieve.

"You look lovely. Breakfast has about five more minutes," he said. "I hope you don't mind, but I had the table on the patio set up."

"That sounds perfect. It's such a nice morning. Do you need my help with anything?"

"No. Let's go outside. Can I get you a mimosa or just orange juice?"

"A mimosa would be great," she said. She was so calm and collected. Honestly, he'd never seen this side of her. Even the day they'd met she'd been fiery, ready to confront him for his rude remark about her to the press.

He walked ahead of her to the French doors and held them open for her. She gave him a tight smile as she walked by, and in that moment, he had a flash of what felt like déjà vu. But he knew it was a childhood memory of his mother treating his father the same way.

Leo felt something inside him die. He'd spent all his life trying to emulate his father, trying to be the business titan that August Bisset was. He'd craved that more than anything, but he'd always thought he was better than his father. Better at treating the people—the women—in his life with kindness and respect. And until this morning, he might have been.

But he'd used Danni as a distraction from the pain and confusion that had plagued him since his parents' secrets were announced, and now he was realizing the cost. He'd done damage that there wasn't an easy way to undo.

And since he was walking out of her life today, he knew that he couldn't really undo it. He was going to have to live with the fact that he'd caused that tight smile. That she'd put up a barrier with those extra-fine manners and the polite small talk that he had no doubt was waiting for him at her breakfast table.

Fuck him.

He wasn't just the son who should have been the heir to Bisset Industries, he was also the same lover who left behind more collateral damage than he'd realized. And that hurt more than Leo would have guessed.

He reached for the champagne, but honestly, did she even want to have breakfast with him? He was tempted to leave, but he hadn't yet decided that he was going to be this much of his father's mini-me. Was there a way to fix this?

He was going to try. He couldn't offer her anything else as a man, but maybe as a business mentor, he could help out. It wasn't much, but it might be enough to make him feel better about the morning.

But he doubted anything was going to fix the hurt he'd caused.

Thirteen

Danni kept her back stiff and her dignity around her, but at this point she had to wonder what had happened to her pride. He'd asked her if she was with him because of who he was when they'd been in bed together as if he didn't know her at all. As if her business meant nothing.

"I can't stop thinking about what you said to me."

"Which part?"

Which part? Oh, this was harder than she'd expected. This was veering away from taking what she needed for her business and into personal territory that would leave her scarred.

"Was I with you because you were a Bisset?"

"Oh, that."

She raised both eyebrows at him, waiting for him to continue.

"I can be an asshole. But you knew that when we met. You wanted me to mentor you. And I don't know what more I can do."

Clearly, he thought that he was better than her. Did she really want business advice from a man who had that kind of mind-set?

"You know, I can't do this," she said. "I think you should just leave."

He stared at her for a long moment and then nodded and pushed himself back from the table. "The food will be done in five minutes. I set the timer on the microwave. I'm sorry. I was trying to make this easier. If you ever need me for anything…or if you are pregnant, please let me know."

If she was pregnant?

"I'm not going to be pregnant. I'm on the pill," she said.

"It's not one hundred percent infallible, and I don't want to follow in my father's footsteps and show up at a wedding thirty years from now and learn we had a kid," he said.

"That won't happen. I'll let you know if there's a kid," she said.

She was reeling, her emotions so out of control in this moment. First he was worried she'd been with him because of his family connections, and now this.

She wasn't sure what she'd expected from Leo, but once again, he'd surprised her. And not in a good way. But still, she couldn't necessarily blame him for making sure that the pregnancy issue was out in the open.

"Thanks," he said.

She stood up and followed him through her rented cottage. The smell of food cooking filled the air, as well as the faintest scent of his cologne. He paused on the threshold with the door open and turned to her, the empty street behind him.

"I really did enjoy this weekend with you, Danni. I'm sorry that I'm not better at easing out of your life," he said. "It was never my intention to hurt you."

She nodded. Hurt her? Had he? Of course he had. She'd known all along that realistically this wasn't going to last, but there had been a part of her that had hung on to hope. Probably the same part of her that wanted to keep her business small but make a huge profit. "Of course. I'm not hurt. We said this was for the weekend. I had a good time, too. Take care."

She sort of shoved him lightly out the door and shut it before her throat closed over the lies she'd told. She thought she'd kept her lawyer's face on the entire time until she caught a glimpse of herself in the mirror in the hallway and realized from her pale complexion she hadn't. She'd never been good at hiding her emotions, and that was especially true with Leo. She hated that.

The timer on the microwave started chirping, and she went to turn off the oven and take out the casserole his grandmother's butler had prepared for them.

God.

If she needed further proof that they weren't meant to be together, there it was. Her grandmother lived in a trailer park in central Florida and drove a golf cart to play bingo and swim with her friends. She didn't have a butler who took food to her grandkids. Her family were lawyers and they made a good living but it wasn't this kind of wealthy. And her family…well, they didn't keep secrets like the Bissets. Her family talked things out, all things, even when they were uncomfortable. Danni had been dabbling with someone whose life was so different from hers that it was no wonder he'd made that comment about her being with him for his name.

The funny thing was, she *had* sort of been with him because of his business. Which might be the same thing? She didn't want to think too much about that, because her heart knew the truth. She'd been with Leo because she liked him. She was starting to more than like him when he'd woken her up with a goodbye on his lips.

She looked down at the counter and saw the note she'd made of questions to ask him and shook her head. He'd written answers to them all and then left her a piece of advice. To dream bigger.

Would she ever really know him?

No. She wouldn't. He'd been pretty plain about that as he'd walked out the door. She would just have to take his advice and make that work for her. Forget about Leo and all the thoughts and feelings he'd stirred in her.

He'd made her almost believe that she was some otherworldly creature who could be comfortable with her wild, curly hair and independent entrepreneurial spirit…just for a moment before he'd walked away.

She wasn't changing her life based on a man who'd done that.

She needed to change her life based on her own opinions. What did she want? Where did she see herself going? She had to make a profit this year—a big one. She decided she'd go to the wedding brunch today and make those connections she'd ignored yesterday because she'd been giving in to the need to be with Leo.

Today, she was a different woman.

He had changed her, she realized. He'd shown her that business and pleasure didn't mix, but pleasure could certainly distract her.

She made a plan for the people she needed to talk to before they left Nantucket and then followed some advice her father had given her long ago— she pictured the meetings in her head, imagined her prospective partners inviting her to collaborate with them and submit her products for a pop-up in their retail chains.

An hour later, when she walked into the banquet room at the Nantucket Hotel, she had that vision firmly in her head, and though her steps faltered when she heard Leo's laugh across the room, she completely ignored him as she sought out the people who could make a real impact on her life.

Not a man whom she'd allowed to distract her from her goals. She wasn't interested in Leo Bisset or anything he had to say. Not anymore. Maybe if she said that enough times in her head, it would actually become the truth and her heart would stop aching at the thought of never seeing him again.

Leo was aware of the moment that Danni entered the banquet hall. He had meant for their break to be clean, and given all his experience with women in the past, he'd sincerely thought that he would be able to ignore her once he walked out her door. But his body hadn't gotten the memo and wasn't interested in ignoring her. His skin felt too tight and his blood felt like it was rushing heavier in his veins as he watched her move through the sparse crowd. He saw her turn to speak to Martha Dillion, a buyer for a large retail chain and Tad Williams's first cousin, but all he could focus on was how with her hair pulled back, her neck seemed so long. He remembered how it had tasted when he'd kissed her there.

Which made him harden, and he had to adjust his stance to avoid anyone else noticing. With perfect timing, Dare walked over to him just then. His oldest brother usually had an air of almost uptight dignity about him, but today he seemed…well, more relaxed, and almost as if he didn't have any worries. Not like Dare at all.

"Had a good night sleep?" Leo asked his brother.

"Something like that," Dare said, snagging a drink from the passing waiter. "You?"

"Great night, sucky morning," Leo said. But he had no one but himself to blame for that. He could have just left things as they were with Danni and been standing next to her as she worked the room. Which she was doing now. Really working it, as far as he could tell.

She must have found his note. That was a tiny sop for his conscience. He knew no matter what she said that he'd hurt her. And that hadn't been his intention at all. True, he wasn't himself, and he'd been acting out all weekend but with her—with Danni—he'd felt like he'd found some solace. And repaying that with hurt wasn't what he'd wanted.

"How was your morning sucky?"

"It's been the worst," he said. "I had to wrap things up with Danni. Didn't want to put it off until she had to leave. Thought it would be better and more dignified."

"Ha."

"Ha?"

"Dignified? When have you ever given a crap

about that? You must have had another reason," Dare said.

"Whatever," Leo said, but his older brother had him thinking. What had he hoped for? Maybe that she'd say she wanted them to try to figure out how to keep seeing each other? Something he knew wasn't possible because he had a very demanding work schedule and lived in the Hamptons and she lived in Boston.

"Look, are you sure you're not being too impulsive here? The truth about Nick, and how he and Logan are actually twins, has rattled all of us. We're dealing with the kind of family drama that normally we don't have to. We leave that to everyone else," Dare said.

"Do we?" Leo asked. "You don't sound like you."

"Good. I've been spending time with someone who suggested I shake things up."

"A woman?"

"Yes," Dare admitted. "And it was nice not to have to watch my back constantly for a change. She's… well, different. She doesn't care about Dad's scandal, Bisset Industries or how I might vote on any issues."

"She sounds…interesting."

"She is. And I didn't cut things off with her. Life doesn't have to always be cut-and-dried."

"Not in my experience," Leo said. "Dad's, either. I mean, Cora Williams was a loose end he should have tied up a long time ago."

"You think Danni is like Cora? I didn't get that read on her, but I really just exchanged small talk with her."

Danni wasn't anything like Nick's mom. For one thing, Danni would never have had an affair with him if he'd been married. Also she wasn't the kind of woman to let Leo off the hook. He knew if she was pregnant, she'd want him to do his part with their child. And he would do it.

He watched her moving around the room, talking to the legendary American designer Peter Drummond, and he realized that he wouldn't mind if she was pregnant. It would give him an excuse to keep seeing her.

Did he need an excuse?

That felt cowardly to him, and he'd always prided himself on facing his problems like a Bisset. Like a man. Not dodging them. If he wanted to see her again, he should just ask.

"You are staring so hard at her right now," Dare said. "It's a wonder she hasn't turned around."

"I am, aren't I?" Had he screwed up this morning? He knew he hadn't. There was no scenario where the two of them actually could be a couple. He had made the right choice. She had her own business to run and a life of her own back in Boston.

But listing all that didn't lessen the fact that he wished he had the right to go up to her. Put his hand on the small of her back and kiss that spot at the base of her neck that he knew turned her on. He wanted that more than he wanted his next breath.

And if he needed more proof that he'd made the smart choice when he'd ended things with her, there it was. He wasn't going to give up his life to build one with her, and he knew from watching everything that had happened with his parents this weekend that he couldn't ask her to do that, either.

They'd had fun together.

That had to be enough. Because as he watched her throughout the brunch, it was clear to him that she had moved on and was determined to let him know it.

Danni collected a lot of names and information throughout the morning. She maneuvered herself through the crowd the way she should have been doing all weekend. Essie was going to be very happy with the results she'd gotten today.

She knew that part of the reason she'd been so successful was that she'd tried to put as many people between herself and Leo as she could. Still, she was putting her connection to him to good use. Something her sister had always told her to do but that Danni had struggled in the past to actually do.

Adler and Nick seemed to have a rosy glow about them. Danni smiled and waved to her client and friend. Adler waved her over to them. Quinn Murray, who had been producing the televised wedding stuff, was now here as a guest and friend to the bride.

"Congratulations again," Danni said after she hugged them both. "Your wedding was fabulously gorgeous. I can't wait to watch when it airs on television."

"Thank you," Nick said. "Your jewelry added the perfect touch to the day. It looked great on the bridesmaids."

"That's sweet of you to say," she responded.

Nick just nodded and then turned away when his brother Asher tapped him on the shoulder.

"He's not wrong," Adler said. "Your jewelry really was a nice touch, and you were, too. Thank you again for everything you did yesterday. Just coming to the prewedding session... I needed you and you were there. I appreciated it so much."

"That's okay. I'd do it again."

"I'm glad. I hope you and Leo—"

She cut Adler off. "There isn't a me and Leo."

"What did he do?" Adler asked.

"Nothing. We weren't planning to be together forever. It was just a fun weekend fling," Danni said. And if she never had to explain it to anyone again, she'd be eternally grateful.

"Oh. I thought it was...something different after all. I hope you had a good time despite the paparazzi and the reporters here. You really helped to make my wedding special."

"I had a great time," she said. "Thanks again for inviting me and for giving your guests my gift bags."

"I didn't mind. Dad loves the bracelet that was in his. I think he wants you to make some for his next tour," Adler said. "I gave him all your details."

Wow, that would be great, Danni thought.

This wedding had netted more than she'd expected. As she drove her car onto the ferry later that afternoon, she realized she was leaving Nantucket a different woman. She'd learned so much, not only from being with Leo, but from watching how he interacted with everyone. The way he'd shown her how to take pictures and, to some extent, how to take risks.

She wasn't sure she was ready to look back at the sketches she'd made when they'd been together, but she knew she would soon. She wanted to just keep this nice numb insulation around her until she got back home and she could let her guard down.

She sat there on the ferry trying not to remember the last time she'd been on the water…it was on the yacht with Leo, and she knew that was when she'd stopped seeing him as a business rival and started to view him as a man.

A man she'd never thought she'd fall for. But she had. She'd definitely fallen for him over the long weekend.

Essie texted to ask if she wanted to have dinner when she got back to the city, and Danni knew that fooling her friend would be hard. Essie would know that things had gone too far with Leo, but at the same time, she couldn't hide that. She felt the pain of it inside, and it was going to take some time and a lot of work to move past it.

Plus, she had a lot of new information to share with Essie, and they needed to get moving on reaching out to the contacts Danni had made.

It was time to stretch her dreams bigger, just as Leo had recommended, and start making her life her own.

She was going to have to thank him for this someday.

But right now, she still felt too raw. She did take comfort in the fact that if she had her way, he was going to see her name a lot in the future. And she hoped it made him remember what they'd almost had.

She hadn't had the courage to call him a coward, but in her heart, she felt like he had been. That he'd walked away from her without even considering ways to make a relationship work. He hadn't even tried.

God.

Oh, but what if he hadn't cared at all? What if the reason he'd been able to walk away so easily was because she'd been the only one who'd felt anything? He had been pretty plain when he'd said his life was a mess and he was trying to get over it by having a fling with her. He'd said he was rudderless, and she'd made herself the wind in his sails.

That was what she did. Dream small and put herself into someone else's vision instead of creating her own. But as Nantucket faded into the background, she vowed she'd never do that again. If anyone was going to be riding someone's coattails in the future, it would be Leo chasing after her. She wasn't going to let this be the last time he saw her, and when they did see each other again, he'd regret that he ever had her and let her go.

Because the new Danni wasn't someone who led with her heart. She was only going to lead with her head…and business smarts that would leave Leo Bisset in the dust.

Fourteen

After two months of strategy sessions with Essie, growing their supply chain and hiring and firing artisans to satisfy the growing demand, Danni had reached a new milestone: the fashion designer Peter Drummond was interested in her work. He'd contacted her to ask if she'd be interested in submitting some designs for a collaboration to be released next summer.

She hardly ever thought about Leo or the last time she saw him on Nantucket. Of course that was a lie; she saw his ads on billboards and on television all the time. Leo Bisset wasn't just a person, he was a brand, and he was everywhere.

Not that she was going to let that matter. Peter Drummond was interested in her work, so she'd focus on that.

It was the kind of opportunity that would take her business to the next level. She now had a good stable of artists working with her to create high-quality jewelry that would meet the standard for collaborating with America's living design legend. And after speaking to her parents, Danni had decided to sell the expensive townhome she was living in and scale down her lifestyle so that she could pump money into her business and ultimately live on the profits alone. It had been a difficult conversation to have, but she had told them frankly she was going to invest in herself. She believed in her jewelry business and wasn't willing to take a back seat on it.

They were encouraging and suggested she rent out her townhome instead of selling it—that way she'd have it when she was back earning what she'd made practicing law. She liked the idea, and once they knew she was serious and wasn't looking to them to support her as she dabbled in her art, it changed the dynamic between them. Danni admitted that even though she was just months away from thirty, it had been the first time she'd actually felt like an adult with her parents. She knew taking responsibility for her own life and decisions had played a huge part in it.

She also admitted to herself that it was Leo who

had given her the drive to make the change. A big part of her wanted to be so successful that he was constantly reminded of her. She'd taken her vision bigger, which had made her focus smaller in so many ways. She knew what she wanted, and that had made her stop chasing trends and fast fashion. As a result, she'd gained the clientele she'd always wanted.

In finding herself as a businesswoman, she realized that she missed Leo, too. It had just been a weekend, and she was trying to remind herself of that, but she knew that she really cared for him. It had taken her about two weeks to admit that she was a bit heartbroken. She'd spent another two weeks obsessively stalking him on social media before she'd mentally slapped herself and stopped that masochistic behavior.

He'd sent her a few texts, which she had longed to read and respond to, but had refused to let herself. A clean break was the last gift he'd given her, and that had to be enough. Still, she'd fashioned the shell he'd found on the beach into a charm for a bracelet. As a base, she used one of the leather bands from his signature line. She'd cut the leather to add in a ribbon that suited her personality and then threaded the ribbon through the shell.

She only wore the bracelet on her days off at first, afraid to let Essie see it because for Danni it was so bittersweet. It combined her and Leo's work, reminding her of when they were at their best, walking together on the beach on Nantucket. But that wasn't reality, she thought as she boarded the flight to New York the day of her big meeting with Peter Drummond's team. While she was in town, she also planned to have lunch with Adler, who wasn't finding married life to be as easy as she'd hoped.

Nick and Logan were at war again thanks to some of Logan's actions before he'd known that Nick was his twin. And scandal still seemed to dog the Bissets, as the board of Bisset Industries required all the Bisset children to have a DNA test to prove they were August's children. Danni had almost texted Leo then. She knew how much he prided himself on being a Bisset, and that had to have stung.

But in the end, he'd made the break with her, and she hadn't reached out. She was trying to be okay with what he'd left her with—after all, Leo had made her stronger in so many ways. She had new business skills that had impressed even her family. She had new connections that she'd been using to the best of her ability. She had learned that business was better when it *was* personal. Those handwritten notes she'd sent after the wedding to tell each of those buyers and designers how nice it was to meet them had paid off.

But that had been her. She'd realized that she couldn't be coldhearted when it came to business. Her products were a reflection of her, and once she and Essie had figured that out, everything else had fallen into place.

In a way, even the sadness she felt when she thought about Leo had made her stronger. She was determined to succeed if for no other reason than to make him have to remember her and their time together.

But in the end, she had to admit that it all added up to one stark truth: as hard as she'd tried to forget him, she hadn't been able to.

She still woke in the night reaching for him, but the bed next to her was empty and cold. She still felt the brush of his lips against hers, which left her mouth tingling and craving a kiss she knew she'd never experience again.

And her hair brought back the worst memories. She'd come close to chopping it all off because she remembered him touching it, twirling it around his finger and claiming that he liked that wildness to her.

In the end she'd taken to wearing it in a tight, low bun at the back of her neck. She didn't want to risk her heart being that vulnerable again, and somehow, the more he'd seemed to accept her secret hidden self, the easier it had been to fall for him.

She wanted to believe she was stronger and would never do that again. And she'd almost convinced herself—until she walked into the Drummond Designs reception area and saw Leo standing there in a suit and tie. In that moment, she knew that all the tight buns and hard talk had just been a facade.

She still cared about Leo; in fact, it was getting

harder to deny that she loved him. No matter how badly he'd hurt her when he'd ended things with her.

The last two months had been hectic and life-changing for Leo and his entire family. His business had been his safe haven. More and more, he'd found himself questioning what he wanted out of life as he watched his parents navigate through the mistakes they'd both made.

One thing that had struck him when he'd had dinner with them last weekend was that they were both committed to each other. The scandals they'd endured had left them stronger together, and he wanted that. As much as he'd at one time believed he was a chip off the August Bisset block and then had hated that he was anything like his father, he now realized that his father had accidentally done the one thing that truly mattered when he'd married Leo's mom.

He wondered if he only believed that because he missed Danni. It was funny to think of how close he'd grown to her over the long weekend, but he knew he'd been more himself with her than with any other person, including his family.

He'd texted her once and she hadn't responded, which was fine. It had stung, but that was her prerogative. He knew he'd been the one to make a clean break, but forgetting her was harder than he'd imagined, and after a night out drinking with his brothers before Zac had to head to Australia to start training for the America's Cup, he'd drunk texted her again.

But that also had gotten no reply, and he'd decided he needed to man up and move on. He knew he'd hurt her, and he guessed that it was the kind of wound she wasn't interested in letting him try to heal. He didn't blame her at all…well, maybe a little, but only because he wanted her back.

So when Peter Drummond had mentioned a collaboration for the coming summer campaign, Leo had done something that wasn't like him at all. Or rather, wasn't like the old Leo. He'd suggested that Drummond take a look at Danni's online portfolio and perhaps invite her to contribute some ideas. He knew he'd be presenting designs as well, and he'd hoped that Drummond would be impressed by Danni. Impressed enough that he'd call them both in about the collab.

And the designer was impressed. *Very* impressed. He'd let Leo know that he thought in a few years she'd be serious competition for Leo. He couldn't help but feel a small sense of pride at all that Danni had accomplished since they'd met. But he also wasn't about to make it easy for her. He was still a businessman who liked to win.

So, when he got to Drummond Designs' offices early for the meeting where the project parameters would be rolled out for the competing designers, he was ready to see Danni and make an impression. To make their business personal. He'd worn his best suit, had his hair trimmed the day before, and he knew he looked good. This was his last chance to try to make amends for how he'd ended things and ask her for a second chance.

He was sober and ready to face her as Leo Bisset. Not the arrogant man he'd been on Nantucket, but a more realistic version of himself. He was no longer just driving himself and his business higher, he was taking steps to make sure that he was going after goals that actually resonated with him.

He'd stopped working seven days a week and had found he liked the downtime. Of course, it had sharpened the ache left by the absence of Danni in his life. And it made him realize that Boston and the Hamptons weren't that far apart.

In his head he had a few ideas of how he wanted this meeting to go. She'd see him, their eyes would meet and she'd run into his arms, confessing that she never should have let him end things.

It was a nice daydream, and a part of him knew that was never going to happen.

But until he turned and saw her standing in the Drummond Designs reception area, he hadn't truly realized how deeply he'd fallen for her. And he was never going to settle for anything other than getting her back into his life.

She had her glorious hair pulled back in a bun, like she had their last morning together. She wore a pencil skirt that hugged the curve of her hips, a flowy blouse with a tie at the neck and heels that made her almost his height. She gave him a smile that he could see was forced. She clearly hadn't expected to see him here today.

He had the advantage, because of course, he'd known she would be. He walked over to her and held his hand out for a handshake.

"Danni, hello, it's good to see you again," he said.

"Leo. I didn't realize you would be here," she said. "But Mr. Drummond did mention there would be other designers submitting work."

"I'm glad he selected you to be one of them," Leo said. "I've been impressed with your new designs."

"Thanks," she said.

"You're welcome," he replied.

She was businesslike and almost a little cold toward him. He knew that he'd hurt her by the way he'd ended things, but had he done too much damage? He didn't have a lifetime bond to fall back on the way his parents had. Was there a chance that he wouldn't win Danni back?

He knew there was that possibility, but he refused to even give it credence. He'd overcome a lot of stuff, and winning Danni back wouldn't be easy, but it was one fight he was going to win.

She knew it would be rude to refuse to shake his hand, but as soon as their fingers brushed, she realized it was a mistake to think she could touch him even in this business setting and not feel that tingle all through her body.

She'd had too much time away from him, and the anger that had kept her back stiff on that Sunday morning at the brunch was no longer driving her. She was sad that he looked so good and she still wanted him as much as she did, even knowing he didn't want her. She was excited to see him again, too. Ready to show she could compete with him and maybe best him, but she also wanted to talk to him. Tell him all the things she'd been doing with her business and catch up on what he'd been doing.

She heard more people entering behind them and tried to step back, but Leo kept hold of her hand.

"Have a drink with me after this meeting," he said.

He wasn't asking, not really, but she knew if she said no he'd let her go. A part of her wanted to make this a second chance. She knew what she wanted in her life now, and she wondered if Leo could fit into that plan. She hadn't been consciously thinking of him but now that he was here, she knew it was going to be so much harder to pretend that she was over him.

"Okay. But I'm not sure when this will end," she admitted.

"Normally Drum is a big fan of a showy presentation, and then he'll ask everyone to go away and come back with some designs," Leo said.

"Good to know," she said.

"Want to sit with me?" he asked.

She frowned. Did he think they were just going to go back to how they'd been before he told her it was over? Did he think that she had been waiting for him to come back into her life? She needed to know where his head was. She didn't want to spend the entire meeting just sitting there thinking about damned Leo Bisset instead of this important collaboration that she wanted. She turned and gestured for him to follow her into the hallway so they'd be alone.

"What are you doing?" she asked. "Why are you acting all chummy?"

He reached up to rub the back of his neck, and his expression tightened. "I was trying to gauge how things were between us."

"Dude, you broke up with me and then offered me business advice. How do you think things are?"

"Well, I don't know, do I? I screwed up, Danni. I was afraid of dragging you into my family mess that I needed to sort out myself. I was also afraid that I was just using you as an escape to forget the mess that was going on."

Those words hurt, but it wasn't as if she hadn't had those same thoughts. "Exactly, that's why I want to know what you are doing. I need to pay attention in the meeting and not be thinking about you and how good you look today and how I'm not sure what 'having a drink' later means to you. Is it something more, or do you just want to get laid again? I don't want to be on that hamster wheel, Leo."

He cursed under his breath and turned away from her for a moment before turning back. His eyes were so blue and bright in his dark face, his expression a mix of emotions that she couldn't read but looked like anger or maybe something else.

"I don't want that for you," he said. "Seeing you today reminded me that in trying to avoid making the same mistakes as my father, I may have made an even bigger one. I don't want to distract you during the meeting, so if you'd like we can skip drinks and wait until after Drummond has made a decision to talk. But know this, Danni—I regret what I did on Nantucket. I'm sorry I hurt you, and I want a chance to start again."

Start again?

The words were still lingering in her mind when Mr. Drummond's assistant came to call them into the meeting. Leo gestured for Danni to go in front of him, and when she got into the meeting room, she saw that there were at least ten other people there. She took a seat, and Leo took one on the other side of the table away from her.

She tried to pay attention to the presentation, but she couldn't. She didn't want to be that kind of woman, but Leo had said things she couldn't just ignore. He had regrets—which part? Ending things with her or sleeping with her?

The lights dimmed, and a film started. She pulled her notebook out, flipped to a blank page and forced herself to try to make notes. And ignore Leo, though it was hard. Why was he doing this? Was he toying with her?

Her gut said no, but the last time she'd trusted it, she'd woken up to a fully dressed Leo, who was trying to make a quick exit from her life, all while telling her he'd do right by her if she had a kid. So she was confused. And angry. And not about to take this quietly, as she suspected that Leo might want her to.

When the film ended, Peter Drummond walked to the center of the room. He was over six feet tall and had a leonine mane of white hair. He also had one of those long handlebar mustaches but it was jet black. His eyebrows were sleek and his face showed signs of his age but not too much. He had an easy smile, which he flashed to the room.

"Thank you all for coming in today. Sorry I was so vague in my invitation but I wanted you to come to this fresh. Now that you've seen the film I hope it's clearer what I'm after."

Danni glanced down at her notebook, which was empty. The film had consisted of images of couples running through fields of high grass and riding horses down a beach. There had been footage of a man diving into an infinity pool that overlooked the Adriatic. So no, it wasn't clear what he was look-ing for.

Leo nudged her arm and showed her his note-pad, which had a big question mark drawn on it. She smiled, glad to see she wasn't the only one not sure what Peter was looking for.

She raised her hand.

"No need for hands here, Ms. Eldridge."

"Um, okay. I'm not entirely sure what you're look-ing for. I have an idea of the feelings you want the campaign to evoke but that's about it."

"Yes. That's it precisely. I want you to tap into the next big thing. I'm afraid if I tell you what I think it is, you'll be limited. I want every part of this project to feel fresh and new."

"What about price point?" Leo asked. "Are you going for the luxury market as you have in the past or are you going to try for the mass market again like your last campaign?"

"A great question," Peter said. "Don't put limits on your designs. Bring me what you want to create."

Again not very direct but Danni wouldn't say it was completely useless. Peter had a chaotic energy and joy that she liked. There was something about him that seemed to want to be surprised.

"Any other questions?"

She shook her head as an idea started to take shape in the back of her mind.

"No. This has been very interesting, Peter. I can't wait to get to my studio," Leo said.

There were similar comments made by the other designers and Danni looked over at Leo, who smiled at her. Something entered her mind, a trigger of a memory from when they'd been together on his yacht, and she knew that would be her inspiration. As unsure as she was of why Leo was back in her life, she had really learned more from him than she realized. He'd showed her a glimpse into a world that she'd never been a part of before.

By the time the meeting finished, she had no idea what she would submit, but she was determined that her design would stand out. Leo was one of the last to leave the meeting room, which she knew, because she'd waited for him in the hallway. It was time for Leo Bisset and her to have a talk. One where she wasn't just forcing a smile and doing the "nice girl" thing.

Fifteen

Leo hadn't meant to unload on Danni before the meeting, and as soon as he saw her waiting for him in the hallway, he knew he'd screwed up again. Why was it with this one woman he never got it right? He wanted to be his best self around her, and instead it seemed as if he was always his worst.

She didn't look that happy to see him, and he realized that he might have blown his last shot to win her back.

"I'm sorry."

"About?"

"Everything," he said. "Come on. There's a coffee shop in the lobby. We can talk there, or I have a car waiting. We can sit in there and talk if you want more privacy."

"The coffee shop sounds good," she said.

So she didn't want to be alone with him, and he couldn't truly say he blamed her. She'd been asking him to just set her mind at ease so she wouldn't be distracted in the meeting, and he'd been unable to do that.

He wanted to tell her that it wasn't his fault. She went to his head and everything got jumbled inside him, and truly it seemed like the harder he tried to make things right, the more they went wrong. Was there ever another person in his life that he'd been this way with?

He knew the answer was no.

Why? he wondered as she stood silently next to him waiting for the elevator to arrive.

When it did, she stepped on and punched the lobby button angrily. And right then, he knew that this wasn't a conversation they could have in public. He wanted to lay his cards on the table, tell her how he really felt and let her tell him everything on her mind. He got on, took her arm and led her back out toward the emergency stairs. He opened the door and pulled her into the stairwell.

"Leo. What the hell are you doing?" she demanded.

"We can't do this in the lobby coffee shop. Paparazzi are still following me around, and I don't think you want pictures of us talking about this splashed on gossip sites," he said.

"Okay, but you could have said something," she said.

"Good. I'm glad," he said, feeling a sense of relief that she was still there with him and hadn't fled the stairwell.

"So what is it you want, Leo? We can't just stand here staring at each other," she said after a moment.

"Who knows when it comes to me and you? I didn't mean to say everything I did earlier. You just go to my head, Danni. I always start out with a plan that seems to go out the window as soon as I'm close enough to smell your perfume or see that small birthmark on the side of your neck just under your ear.

"Then I stop thinking and my most primal self takes over and I have to get you back. Why did I ever let you go? And that's not rational, is it? We only spent a weekend together, and my life was complete chaos during it, but I truly feel like being with you was the realest thing about that time. That our time together saved me. I can't figure it out, but being away from you has only made me want and need you more. And that's not normally how I am. I think... hell, I don't think, I know that I love you, and I can't figure out if we can ever make a life together work because we've never tried it, but at the same time I know—like, down in my soul—that I can't live without you."

She just stood there looking up at him, blinking, and then she shook her head. "You love me?"

"I do," he said. "I was afraid that what I felt on Nantucket was just a reaction to you being the only bright spot in that weekend for me. But I've known for weeks now that I love you, and I'm going to do everything I can to prove it to you and win you back."

"You love me."

She just spoke the words back to him as if she wasn't sure if he was playing a game or not.

"Yes."

"Now you tell me, when I'm trying to get over you and prove that I'm not running after you and following your lead? Now you tell me, when I have the chance to get a big brand deal and finally get my business off the ground?"

"Yes."

"Leo Bisset, you suck," she said. "I hate that you said you love me now when I'm still mad at you. I'm not ready to hear those words when I'm busy thinking about how I'm going to kick your ass in the presentation and win this client. But now I can't do that, can I? Because I love you, too. I hate that I haven't been able to write you off as a wedding weekend hookup. I thought you didn't care about me at all."

"I care too much," he said. "I didn't want to be like my father and drag you into a lifetime of ups and downs. Over the past few months, I finally figured out what I want in my life, and it's you. If I have to give up this collab, I will. If you say move to Boston and we can try dating, I will. If you say you never want to see me again…"

She just stood there watching him, her brown eyes full of emotions that he wished he could read but couldn't. He knew that he had to be able to let her go if he had any chance of making this work. He had realized while they were apart that love wasn't a one-sided, get-your-own-way-every-time thing, it was a selfless emotion that meant putting her first.

He loved her so much that her happiness mattered to him in ways he was only beginning to comprehend.

"You won't see me again?" she asked. This was it, she thought. The moment when she'd know for sure how he really felt. She felt like she was seeing ratty-canvas-shoes Leo. The real Leo and not the smooth, sophisticated man she'd spent the afternoon watching during the presentation.

This was the man she'd fallen in love with, she realized. The man who'd answered her business questions on that note in the cottage kitchen without show or fanfare because, at his heart, Leo Bisset was a good guy. He worried too much about following in his father's footsteps and leaving behind messes that would have to be dealt with thirty years in the future, when in reality he'd never do that.

He was too caring.

"It will kill me, but if that's what you truly want, I'll do it," he said. "I can't imagine that even if you never saw me again, I will ever stop loving you."

She nodded.

The gesture was more for herself than him, but when he sighed, she knew he'd taken it to mean she never wanted to see him again. He turned away, but she put her hand over his, turning him back to face her.

"Thank you for being willing to give me the space I need, but what I really want is a life with you. A way to figure out if this can work. I love you, too. I've spent the last two months trying to forget you and realizing that I never will. Like you said, I'm not sure that we can merge our lives together, but I truly want to try. I've been living with the ghost of you for these last months and that's not enough.

"I looked at that note you left me and tried to dream bigger because of you. I've made huge changes in my life, but the truth is without you in the picture, my dream was only half-real. And it could never actually come true. I don't want you to think I need you to complete me or anything like that, but having you by my side rounds out the life I'm making. I'd rather come to this realization now than spend the rest of my life regretting that I didn't take a chance on love when I could."

He pulled her into his arms and lowered his head to kiss her. He tasted better than she remembered, and she wrapped her arms around his shoulders and clung to him. Happiness overwhelmed her; she'd never dared to think she'd be able to have him back in her life. And on her terms...well, their terms.

He stepped back. "We need to get out of here. I have an apartment in the city. Would you come with me? I want to make love to you and then figure out our future."

"There's nothing I'd rather do," she said, reaching out and taking his hand in hers. As she did so, the sleeve of her blouse fell back, revealing the bracelet she'd made from his leather band and the shell he'd found on the beach.

He lifted her wrist and looked at it. "I didn't know you had made this. This is us, isn't it? A mixture of my business and yours, but also the start of our life together."

"It is, though I didn't realize it when I made it. I thought this would be a reminder not to let my heart get involved in business decisions, but it has turned out to be my good-luck talisman when I make deals."

"It has?"

"Yes," she admitted. Though she hadn't wanted it to be true, looking back, the bracelet had given her the confidence to pursue her dreams. And it had represented their love when Leo wasn't with her.

"I have an idea for the collaboration. How do you feel about working with me instead of competing?"

"I'm listening," she said.

"First things first," he said as he led her back into the hallway to the elevators. He didn't say a word as they rode down to the ground floor. When the elevator doors opened, he quickly ushered her through the lobby to his waiting car.

When they got back to his apartment, Leo carried her to his bedroom and made love to her. He took his time making sure she realized how much she meant to him. He had missed her more than he realized and though he wanted to go slowly, he found he couldn't. But she was just as hungry for him.

Afterward, as she lay in his arms, he outlined his idea to take her bracelet and use it as the jumping-off point for his-and-hers bracelets for the Drummond collection. They both knew it would be a winner.

But it wasn't the business idea that was keeping them together.

It was their love for each other.

Adler was a bit surprised when Danni brought Leo to their lunch meeting. But as soon as she saw her friend and her cousin together, she saw why. No matter how much heartache she'd had at her wedding, and from the ongoing issues involving the rivalry between the Williams and Bisset families, at least Zac and Leo had found love. Logan had, too, and despite the chaos he'd caused for Nick and his business, she was happy for him and Quinn. But Adler's new husband was putting in a lot of extra

hours, thanks to Logan's sneaky buying of that patent company.

"Well, hello, you two," she said, forcing a smile,
determined to keep up the facade of happy new wife,
even though her existence now revolved around
dodging the paparazzi and trying to keep her husband from ruining the new life she wanted for them.

"Hello, Adler," Leo said, coming over and giving
her a warm hug. "I hope it's okay that I came. I know
there's a lot of tension between Nick and our family
these days. But I miss you, so I decided to try to tag
along. If you want me to go, I will."

She hugged him back, realizing how much she'd
missed her cousins since she'd gotten back from her
honeymoon and everything had blown up between
Nick and Logan. "I'm happy to see you, too. Are the
two of you together? When did that happen?"

"At your wedding," Danni said. "But you knew
that. We just got back together a few days ago."

"And it's good?"

"Yes," Leo said. "It's really good. Like you and
Nick."

She hoped it wasn't like her and Nick. Things had
really deteriorated between them. She wanted better
for her cousin and Danni. But Adler realized that she
was going to take steps to get her marriage back on
track. If that meant telling Nick how she really felt
about his feud with her cousins, then so be it. She

was tired of trying to keep the peace when no one else seemed interested in that.

Danni's and Leo's phones both pinged, and they turned to look at their screens. Then they glanced at each other with secret smiles and love in their eyes.

"Good news?"

"Yes. We've both been chosen to do a big-time collaboration with Drummond Designs," Danni said.

"This calls for champagne," Leo said. He got up to go find their waiter.

When he was gone, Danni leaned in closer. "I would never have guessed that I'd be this in love with Leo Bisset."

"I'm glad to hear it. He's a good man. And you two met because of me. I'm taking all the credit," Adler said, winking at Danni. She forced herself out of her funk because she was so happy to see the two of them in love.

She suspected it wouldn't be long until they were collaborating on more than just designs.

* * * * *

#2869 STAKING A CLAIM

Texas Cattleman's Club: Ranchers and Rivals • by Janice Maynard

With dreams of running the family ranch, Layla Grandin has no time for matchmaking. Then, set up with a reluctant date, Layla realizes he sent his twin instead! Their attraction is undeniable but, when the ranch is threatened, can she afford distractions?

#2870 LOST AND FOUND HEIR

Dynasties: DNA Dilemma • by Joss Wood

Everything is changing for venture capitalist Garrett Kaye—he's now the heir to a wealthy businessman *and* the company's next CEO. But none of this stops him from connecting with headstrong Jules Carson. As passions flare, will old wounds and new revelations derail everything?

#2871 MONTANA LEGACY

by Katie Frey

After the loss of his brother, rancher Nick Hartmann is suddenly the guardian of his niece. Enter Rose Kelly—the new tutor. Sparks fly, but with his ranch at stake and the secrets she's keeping, there's a lot at risk for them both...

#2872 ONE NIGHT EXPECTATIONS

Devereaux Inc. • by LaQuette

Successful attorney Amara Devereaux-Rodriguez is focused on closing her family's multibillion dollar deal. But then she meets Lennox Carlisle, the councilman and mayoral candidate who stands in their way. He's hard to resist. And one hot night together leads to a little surprise neither expected...

#2873 BLACK TIE BACHELOR BID

Little Black Book of Secrets • by Karen Booth

To build her boutique hotel, socialite Taylor Klein needs reclusive hotelier Roman Scott—even if that means buying his "date" at a charity bachelor auction. She wins the bid and a night with him, but will the sparks between them upend her goals?

#2874 SECRETS OF A WEDDING CRASHER

Destination Wedding • by Katherine Garbera

Hoping for career advancement, lobbyist Melody Conner crashes a high-profile wedding to meet with Senator Darien Bisset. What she didn't expect was to spend the night with him. There's a chemistry neither can deny, but being together could upend all their professional goals...

HDCNM0322

A sharp rap on her door startled Arlie out of her misery.

"Just a minute!" she called, twisting off the shower.

Opening the shower door, she slid into one of the complimentary plush robes, then gathered the long skein of her hair and squeezed the water out of it with a towel before draping it over her shoulder.

Good enough for food delivery. She exited the bathroom in a cloud of steam and pulled open the propped door.

Samuel Kane's face appeared in the gap.

Only he didn't look like Samuel Kane.

He looked like wrath in a Brooks Brothers suit. Jaw set, the muscles flexed, mouth a thin, grim line. Eyes blazing emerald against chiseled cheekbones.

"Oh," she said dumbly. "Hi."

A sinking feeling of self-consciousness further heated her already shower-warmed skin as he stared at her.

"Do you want to come in?" she added when he made no reply. She stepped aside to grant him entry, catching the subtle scent of him as he moved past her into the hallway.

"Why didn't you tell me?" he asked.

Arlie's heart sank into her guts. There were too many answers to this question. And too many questions he didn't even know to ask.

"Tell you what?" she asked, opting for the safest path.

Coward.

Samuel stepped closer, her glowing white robe reflected in icy arcs in his glacier-green eyes. "About my father. About what he said to you this morning."

The wave of relief was so complete and acute it actually weakened her knees.

"Our families have a lot of shared history," Arlie said. "Not all of it good."

"He had no right—"

"I'm sorry," she interrupted, knowing it was a weak and deliberate dodge. She didn't want to talk about this. Not with him. "It's absolutely mandatory that you surrender your tie and suit jacket for this conversation. I'm entirely underdressed and frankly feeling a little vulnerable about it."

Walking into the well-appointed sitting area, Samuel shrugged out of his suit jacket and laid it across the chaise longue. As he turned, they snagged gazes. He gripped the knot of his tie, loosening it with small deliberate strokes that inexplicably kindled heat between Arlie's thighs.

"Better?" he asked.

On a different night, in a different universe, it would have ended there.

But for reasons she could neither explain nor ignore, Arlie padded barefoot across the space between them.

"Almost." Lifting her hands to his neck, she undid the button closest to his collar. Then another. And another.

To her great surprise and delight, Samuel wore no T-shirt beneath.

Dizzy with desire, Arlie tilted her face up to his. The air was alive with electricity, crackling and sizzling with anticipation. The breathless inevitability of this thing between them made her feel loose-limbed and drunk.

"All my life, I could have anything I wanted." Cupping her jaw, he ran the pad of his thumb over her lower lip. "Except you."

Arlie's breath came in irregular bursts, something deep inside her tightening at his admission. "You want me?"

Samuel only looked at her, silent but saying all.

His wordlessness the purest part of what he had always given her.

The look that passed between them was both question and answer.

Yes?

Yes.

Don't miss what happens next in…
Corner Office Confessions
by USA TODAY *bestselling author Cynthia St. Aubin.*

Available May 2022 wherever
Harlequin Desire books and ebooks are sold.

Harlequin.com

HDEXP0322

Get 4 FREE REWARDS!

We'll send you 2 FREE Books plus 2 FREE Mystery Gifts.

FREE Value Over **$20**

Both the **Harlequin® Desire** and **Harlequin Presents®** series feature compelling novels filled with passion, sensuality and intriguing scandals.

Love Harlequin romance?

DISCOVER.

Be the first to find out about promotions, news and exclusive content!

f Facebook.com/HarlequinBooks

y Twitter.com/HarlequinBooks

O Instagram.com/HarlequinBooks

P Pinterest.com/HarlequinBooks

You Tube YouTube.com/HarlequinBooks

ReaderService.com

EXPLORE.

Sign up for the Harlequin e-newsletter and download a free book from any series at **TryHarlequin.com**

CONNECT.

Join our Harlequin community to share your thoughts and connect with other romance readers!
Facebook.com/groups/HarlequinConnection

HSOCIAL2021